BACK TO THE DRAWING BOARD

PETER CLEVERLY

BOOKHOUSE
publishing

Published by

Bookhouse Publishing

4 Aspall Road

Debenham

Suffolk

IP14 6QA

© 1997 Bookhouse Publishing

Designed and printed in Great Britain by

Fieldfare Publications, Cambridge.

ISBN 0 9527355 2 0

Back to the Drawing Board

Contents

I

A Rank Outsider.

At the heart of the county of Suffolk is the wool town of Lavenham and at the heart of Lavenham, like a genial and manipulative old spider is Sir Hastings Munro, an architect of much distinction and having many old fashioned virtues (old fashioned vices besides). Subordinate to this rotund and impressive figure are three assistants, to say nothing of his acerbic secretary. His three assistants are headed by Ron Steel, now well into his sixties and, from goodness knows when, Sir Hastings' right hand and the other two, nominally equal (but actually in practical terms subordinate), Byam Alexander and myself, Jack Simpson. A more unlikely team it would be hard to imagine. I am plodding and deliberate and pathologically anxious; Byam is confident, flamboyant and a chancer. Ron is omniscient! Through the three years in which we have been together he has guided our faltering steps through the exigencies of defaulting clients, scoundrelly builders and structural crises large and small. The wonder is that we have become, and remain, mates.

From time to time during this period Byam and I reminded each other that Sir Hastings had at the outset indicated that each of us was likely to be considered for a partnership. The tricky old devil had written to us individually on acceptance of our application for the post of assistant ending with the teasing words - '...you may regard the coming three years as a period of trial with a view to a partnership.' Absurd as it may seem, neither of us had quite liked to remind him of this. His memory was fugitive at the best and he was skilled in extricating himself from any conversation his quick senses warned him to avoid but we were both aware of a rising tension and expectation as the three years drew to a close and determined that the subject should be aired. Claire loyally insisted that Hastings was no fool and that he was well aware of the greater value of the work I had put in, of my steadiness in a crisis and of my sense of responsibility. But I thought of Byam, his charm, his style, his flashes of inspiration and I thought of his forthcoming link with the most important building family in the eastern counties and I wondered.

Ron and I, both happily married, have during these years viewed with fascination, exasperation and irritation Byam's many affairs of the heart. At the time, Byam's career seemed to be approaching its apogee as, to the surprise of all, it seemed he had in fact secured the immensely rich and beautiful Gentian Woodruffe, the only daughter of a respected and alarming client and in the third autumn of our contract with Hastings the happy, if quarrelsome, pair announced their engagement.

Dressed in our wedding finery, Claire and I jostled for position, admiring ourselves in the only long glass at 14, the Pottergate.

"Like this? Or like this?" said Claire, trying her hat in this way and that.

"Grey tie or blue tie?" I asked. She took no more notice of me than I had taken of her.

"Byam!" said Claire anxiously. "I do hope he gets there in time!"

We looked at our watches.

"I wouldn't count on it," said I. "When I saw him last - yesterday evening - he seemed to be about half way through a twenty four hour party!"

"Stupid twit! But there we are... Fine day... Happy is the bride and all that..."

"Have we got time to stop in a car wash?"

"No, we're late as it is. God knows what the parking problems will or won't be."

The parking problems were considerable. The Great and Good (many of them chauffeur-driven) were setting down before the Abbey. The bells of St. Edmund were banging away happily, vying with the organ which discoursed a complicated and, in my opinion, annoyingly elaborate snatch of Bach and we took our seats. About half way up, not among the toffs, but then not among the groundlings, it was a nicely calculated comment on our station in life. Glancing ahead and into the first class accommodation, I noted an iron-grey head and the elegant back of a morning coat archaically bound in black silk which turned to reveal the cheerful face of Sir Hastings. A glance to the left revealed our old friend and client Clive Belton looking not at his best within an unsuitable and voluminous checked satin cravat.

"Hey, just a moment," said Claire anxiously. "Are we on the right side? Are we friends of the bride or the bridegroom?"

"Don't care - I detest them both impartially," I muttered. "But - Byam? I can't see him. Where is he?"

I discreetly searched.

"The swine! He's not going to turn up. I knew it! I should have stayed with him last night..."

"Oh Lord, do you think so?" said Claire. "You could be right. I can't say I'd blame him though. It was never going to be easy even for someone with his panache."

At that moment the west doors opened behind us, the Abbey was flooded with light, the organ burst into Widor's Toccata and two black clad gentlemen emerged from the transept and took their place at the altar steps. Well at least the bridegroom and best man were in position. A moment later a dignified figure came stalking up the aisle behind us and stepped into the pew beside Claire. Correctly dressed, it has to be conceded, but that apart, looking as though he had just been fished from the river.

"Bloody hell!" said Byam and Claire took his hand encouragingly.

"You look like Sidney Carton," she said, "delivering his speech from the scaffold."

"This is a far, far, more bloody awful thing I do now than I have ever done," he hissed.

Claire turned about to observe the approach of the bride and Byam and I gazed steelily forward. The bridegroom at the altar turned to the west with a beaming smile. His best man did likewise. On the one hand, Brigadier Molyneux and in support, his cousin, Major General, the Honourable Miles Wedderburn Wentworth.

Floating on the arm of Dennis Woodruffe, Gentian shimmered up the aisle, lovely as a lily in white silk. Dennis Woodruffe, on the other hand, looked as though he had been recently stuffed by an inexpert taxidermist.

This day which seemed to display the best that Suffolk had to offer in the form of magnificent architecture, sparkling spring sunshine, meticulously chosen and well presented music, a very large number of fancily dressed clergy and the full of the racing and military establishment was, in fact, the end product of six months or thereabouts of heart-churning drama.

It was from the Cesarewich the previous October that Byam had returned elated, having finally persuaded Gentian Woodruffe to marry him and finally persuaded her father to vouchsafe his paternal blessing. Happy ending? It seemed so to me. Claire, on the other hand, who had manfully espoused Byam's cause throughout his action-packed courtship, announced when all were sure of a happy conclusion that 'it would never do.' I couldn't think why.

"Why didn't you say so at the time?" I said on more than one occasion.

A question she couldn't answer. She had fostered the romance but then had also introduced the Brigadier to Gentian and Gentian had introduced the Brigadier to her father. Arising from this a happy partnership had been established. A partnership in the service of which the Brigadier had become a frequent visitor at Pitt House, the Woodruffe's establishment between Newmarket and Ely.

As the weeks rolled past, I had become aware of a certain preoccupation on the part of Byam. I had observed the Brigadier, Gentian and Byam doing things together - an incongruous trio. On the few occasions that I saw Dennis Woodruffe it seemed that he too was a prey to preoccupation. It wasn't until Christmas or thereabouts that it became obvious that - as I put it myself - Gentian was about to do the dirty on Byam. The Brigadier, with all the seasoned care of an experienced horseman, had been discreetly coming up on the rails. There ensued a series of heart-broken renunciations, tearful reconciliations, a certain amount of stalking off into the sunset and a very large number of anguished telephone calls at the conclusion of which:-

'Mr. Dennis Woodruffe requests the pleasure of the company of Mr. and Mrs. J. Simpson at the marriage of his daughter Gentian to Brigadier Molyneux... the Abbey... and afterwards at Pitt House... RSVP.'

"Better so," said Claire.

I couldn't see it.

"But he's ancient - what on earth does Gentian see in him?" I had bleated.

"Oh, come on Jack," Claire had replied treacherously (though she would have said with the calm judgement of a pragmatist), "he's not that old! He's a Bosnian brigadier, don't forget, not a World War Two one! Like policemen and

5

pilots - they are young these days. And besides, he's very good looking, he's charming and he happens to be the present owner of what Gentian is pleased to call her 'ancestral home'. And, of course, you can't ignore the shared family interest in racing. No, looked at from any viewpoint it's a very suitable match."

Claire had at this time, through her association with the Woodruffes and the Brigadier, acquired a large number of not perfectly understood racing metaphors, 'Byam'll never be up to the weight over the distance,' amongst them.

"Poor old Byam, though," I said. "It'll break his heart. He's thought about nothing else for a year or more."

"I don't think it will break his heart," said Claire. "Tough old heart. If I know Byam, it won't be long before he's re-equipped himself with a girl - in fact, I'll have a bet with you - I'll go further - I'll give you a hundred to eight he'll be back in business within six months! Besides... nice for the Brig... at his age. He must be all of forty five. Nice to have a young and beautiful wife twenty years younger than himself."

"Bugger the Brig," I said, by no means reconciled to this recent turn of events.

The wedding wound its way onwards as weddings do. We listened to a mellifluously produced anthem, we listened to the apt words of a crimson-faced Archdeacon (a distant connection of the Brigadier's who might have been John Jorrocks himself.) We sang 'Immortal, Invisible, God Only Wise', and, heartened by the noise around me, I dared to venture on the descant but was halted in my inspired rendition by the sight of a tear stealing down Byam's cheek. A tear, I thought, fifty percent generated by genuine grief and fifty percent generated by the two day binge from which he was just emerging.

Claire squeezed Byam's arm comfortingly. "Why don't you give the reception a miss?" she whispered.

"I wouldn't miss it for the world," said Byam and we

shuffled off slowly out of the church in the way one does after weddings and into the sunshine where cameras clicked and onwards to Pitt House.

The day was so fine for the time of year that the reception soon debouched from the house and into the garden. Here we encountered Sir Hastings. Portly and proprietorial, he had on his arm a small, sandy, bright, blue-eyed girl.

"Help!" I said to Claire in alarm. "Whatever next?"

"No, no," she hissed. "It's his niece."

Genial as ever, Sir Hastings waved a glass of champagne (not his first of the day) and came towards us.

"Ah, there you are, my dear chap! There you are! Now let me introduce my niece, Kirsten, well, great niece, you know. Kirsten, this is Jack Simpson and this is his wife Claire."

The bright-eyed Kirsten looked at us, it seemed, without much favour and, having effected the introduction, Hastings wandered away, leaving us together. I'm not good at such occasions but Claire went smoothly into action with the inanities appropriate to such an encounter.

"Your first visit to Suffolk?... Where do you live?... It's a lovely day for a wedding, isn't it?" And, finally, "Er, what do you do?"

"I'm an architect," said Kirsten in the refined accents of Edinburgh. "Didn't Uncle Hastings tell you?"

"No, I don't think so. Did he mention it to you, Jack?"

"No, he hasn't told us anything about his family or what they do."

"That's very typical," said Kirsten composedly and then, "I'm coming to work in his office. I'm starting on Monday."

She turned enquiringly to me and asked, "And what do you do Mr. Simpson?"

Claire and I staggered a bit but explained as best we could who we were and what we did and I cursed Hastings, not for the first time, for his devastating practice of letting not his left hand know what his right hand was

7

doing. So overwhelmed were we by this latest piece of information that the rest of our conversation with Kirsten was stilted and embarrassed and it wasn't until we were in the car and going home that we were able to discuss this remarkable turn of events.

"What an extraordinary thing!" I said. "Now what can the significance of that be? I wonder if she's any good?"

"I thought she looked nice," said Claire, "but I sort of had a feeling she didn't like us much."

"Ah, that's the Scots," I said. "You wouldn't expect a rave notice on two minutes' acquaintance."

"Do you need any more help in the office?"

"Do we ever! I mean, if she's any good, she'll be a godsend but what's Heather going to say?"

"And what's Byam going to say?"

We batted it back and forth and that evening I rang up Byam who received the news with gloom.

"Well, I didn't meet her because I slipped off early but I did spot a little ginger thing hanging on Hastings' arm. And are you telling me that she...? On Monday...? Don't like the sound of this, old boy!" he said bodefully. "I don't like it at all. Know what I think? We're being eased out. This Kirsten's the Crown Princess, can't you see that? And you know what we've been doing? Keeping the bloody job warm for her! The old rascal's been keeping the firm ticking over until she'd qualified! And to think we've been watching each other like hawks for three years! No, I don't like the sound of this at all."

At this juncture, Claire who had been listening to half of the conversation, snatched the receiver from my hand and said crisply, "That's rubbish, Byam! I don't believe a word of it! Besides, I thought she looked very nice."

"Nice!" said Byam. "She may be nice but you know what the Scots are?"

"No, I don't think I know any," said Claire, "apart from Hastings that is but I expect you're going to enlighten me from your vast experience."

"Grasping, acquisitive, unscrupulous, given over to Clan Loyalty and all that and - very clever. Didn't we say it right at the beginning? - 'Wouldn't trust Hastings as far as the end of the garden!'"

But Claire was having none of it. "I think she'll be a very valuable addition," she said. "Keep up behind you both and make sure you don't stray," she added provokingly.

"Humph!" said Byam. "You see her as our sheepdog do you? Not a bit of it! I see her as a border terrier - ginger, yapping and aggressive but she'll be no match for me - the Hound of the Baskervilles!"

II

Sabotage.

And so Kirsten joined the squad. Cool, detached, she stepped calmly into the slot vacated by an unsatisfactory predecessor. I had wondered how Heather would cope with another female under the sacred roof of Spring House. I needn't have worried. Heather saw her as an ally. Heather, Kirsten, Sir Hastings on the one hand, Byam, Ron and me on the other.

Kirsten was meticulous and particular, caustic and dismissive. Without seeming to do so, she kept us all at arm's length.

"Can't make her out," Byam said from time to time.

It was clear to me that his seductive wiles had made no impression on Kirsten, armoured as she was against such things by a trim Scottish propriety. In the end he decided that she was a sister. In real life - as it were - Byam had several younger sisters and Kirsten just increased the tally by one. They developed a camaraderie I was glad to see and, of Byam's many voices, that of Edinburgh was among his best - so good, in fact, that they conversed easily for days in the accents of Morningside before Kirsten realised she was being sent up. Byam enjoyed this game and polished his performance; Kirsten enjoyed it too and even greeted Byam's more outrageous offerings with an austere smile.

Her immediate predecessor had been very odd. In ordinary circumstances I would never have dreamed of taking him on but at the time my morale was at a low ebb. Byam's stormy love life had more or less phased him out for a number of weeks and, indeed, by inattention, he had lost us a valuable job - a shopping mall. A vile, pushy little firm called pretentiously 'The Goldhawke Design and Build Partnership' had sneaked this away from us. I was desperate for some back-up but even so, I should have been warned from the outset just how very odd our new recruit was. There were hints even on the first telephone conversation. Having made an appointment for him to come and see us, I remembered to ask his name. This seemingly innocent question was received with a scornful laugh and he had hung up. After this unpromising beginning I was surprised when he duly appeared for interview.

He was very dark. He had a good deal of bushy hair, a dark complexion and curious yellow eyes. He was wearing a chocolate brown suit, a chocolate brown shirt and a chocolate brown tie. I bent surreptitiously to check whether he was wearing chocolate brown socks. He was. The interview went something like this:-

Self   And where have you been working Mr. Parry? (I had at least established that his name was Christopher Parry.)

Parry   Does it matter?

Self   Well, I would have thought it mattered.

Parry   You're saying you don't know where I've been working?

Self   Well, since you haven't told me, it's hardly likely that I'd know where you'd been working.

Parry   Ah, well, have it your own way but I imagine your friend Charlie has been on the phone.

Self   Charlie?

Parry   (With heavy emphasis) Mr. Boldero if you prefer.

Self   Oh, Charlie Boldero? Is that where you've been?

11

Parry   (Wearily) Yes, that's where I've been.

And more in the same vein.

I had by now decided that however desperate we were in the office for another pair of hands, under no consideration whatever was I going to take Christopher Parry on but he continued:-

"Perhaps you'd like to see some of my work?" and he handed me a large marbled portfolio. In all the circumstances I could hardly refuse to have a look at his work so we laid it out on the table.

It has to be said that Christopher Parry was brilliant. I really don't think I'd ever seen work of such class. Clear, incisive, beautiful lettering, carefully tabulated revisions down the side. I began to change my mind and ask more domestic questions such as when could he start and what sort of salary did he want?

He fielded these questions with an enigmatic smile. He shot me a look from time to time which I can only describe as pitying. He perpetually gave the impression that he knew more than he was saying and that I knew that he knew more than he was saying and that he was not deceived by my seeming prevarication and towards the end of the interview I said, "You won't mind my ringing up Charlie Boldero, I'm sure?"

"Well, you're going to ring him up anyway so it doesn't make much difference what I say."

I blinked a bit at this but, much impressed by his drawing and, I will confess it, intrigued by his mysterious personality, I offered him the job. Grudgingly he said he'd try us out for three months and, glad of this let out clause, I closed with him.

"Of course," he said, "I knew you were going to say that and so long as we both understand each other from the outset there's no reason why it shouldn't work. I'll see you on Monday." And he was gone.

I sprang to the telephone and rang Charlie Boldero.

"Charlie," I said. "Christopher Parry. Mean anything to you?"

"Christopher Parry? Oh, my God! Why do you want to know, Jack?"

"Well, right or wrong, win or lose, I've just offered him a job."

To my consternation Charlie burst into a roar of laughter, "Oh, Good Lord!" he said and over his shoulder I heard him hissing, "Johnny! Jack Simpson's just given old Parrynoia a job!" And there was a good deal of fruity male laughter.

"Oh, come on Charlie! What are you saying?"

I could almost hear Charlie mopping his eyes but he collected himself and said, "Well I suppose the buck has to stop somewhere and... hee, hee, hee... it couldn't have happened to a nicer chap, if you know what I mean!"

"For God's sake, Charlie, come to earth and tell me what you're trying to say!"

"Okay - to be fair to the guy, he can draw like an angel but, and this you will find - he's nuts."

"He's what?"

"Nuts. As you will swiftly find out. I never really managed to unravel all this but he has no doubt at all in his mind that he is pursued."

"Pursued?"

"Yes, pursued. I'm not quite sure who by. Would it be the KGB or Infada? Isn't there something called a Fatwa? Whatever it is, he behaves as though he's just been handed the Black Spot. But it could be just a couple of angry fathers each armed with a paternity order, I suppose. Be it as it may, he has got the archetypal, original, steel-lined, radio-active persecution complex. I didn't get rid of him - he got rid of me! (Mind you I was glad to see the back of him.) He walked out because he thought I was one of THEM. Believe me, Jack, it won't be more than five minutes before you're one of THEM too. Still, you'll get some good work out of him while he lasts. I'll give him six months."

And with this unreassuring prognostication he cut off.

On the due date Christopher Parry appeared and I settled him down to complete the drawings on a large, no-expenses-spared remodelling and extension of a local inn. I established him in a corner of the office where, in addition to a comfortably partitioned off space, he even had a window while the rest of us were dependent on roof lights. He looked suspiciously round his kennel. "What's that building over there?" he said, pointing. I didn't know. "I'll have to find out," he said, making a note on a pad.

His work, though, was distinctly good and his hours-keeping was extraordinary. To Heather's acid irritation he was in the office by half past eight every morning and I can hardly remember a day when he was not working on when I myself went home.

"I don't like it," said Heather. "What's he want to come in so early for? Sneaky, I call it. Poking his nose in everywhere. Caught him going through Byam's drawers yesterday which is more than I'd care to do myself and he's that quizzy you wouldn't believe! Mark my words - we'll all wake up dead in our beds before we know where we are! Serial killer's eyes, that's what he's got!"

I knew what she meant though I reassured her as best I could. The picture of Chris Parry hurrying from Spring House where he'd slain Hastings and Heather and on to Cambridge for Byam and back to the Pottergate for Claire and me through a busy and blood-soaked night was a stimulating one.

Trying to find out more about him I took him with me on a survey but I was wasting my time. He fended off every question with a sly smile and when I expressed mild concern about him he said with much hauteur, "You don't have to worry - I'm quite capable of looking after myself as others have found before you. Anyone who tangles with me lives to regret it."

What on earth could I possibly make of that? I passed this on to Claire on return and, predictably, she began to feel sorry for Christopher Parry. "Parrynoia! Huh!" she said. "That's typical of Charlie Boldero! This poor boy's obviously very troubled. Did you find out anything about his background?"

I confessed that I hadn't.

"Well you should have done. Bring him round to supper one night."

And this, reluctantly, I did.

Christopher Parry, when exposed to the Lucullian luxury of the Pottergate, was a character transformed. He scarcely spoke above a whisper, his eyes were perpetually downcast. He returned embarrassingly humble thanks for everything that was put before him were it a glass of rioja or a second helping of steak and kidney pudding. He managed to give the impression that this was the first time he had been warm for weeks, that he hadn't had a square meal for years and that he was completely unmanned by our condescension in having a creature so despicable within our doors. It was a creepy performance.

By a considerable stroke of luck about half way through what was an increasingly sticky evening, the telephone rang and the yapping, cheerful voice of Hastings came clearly over for all to hear. I knew these evening sessions with Hastings; I knew he himself would have had a jolly good dinner, probably had just poured himself out a second glass of port and wanted nothing so much as someone to talk to for half an hour or so. On the verge of cutting him off, I suddenly thought I'd take this one upstairs and with suitable apology I fled the room. People always unburdened themselves to Claire. If anyone could get to the essence of Christopher Parry it would be Claire but it was obvious that he wasn't going to peel off any layers of personality while I was there.

When I came down, Christopher, with humble thanks was on the point of leaving and, having waved him away, Claire and I turned to contemplate each other. "Well?" we both said with one breath and I added, "Did you get anything?"

Claire shook her head in deep puzzlement and said, "As far as I can see he 'did something' when he was a student in Germany. What he did or thinks he did I have no idea but, as a result of that, he is a victim of an implacable vendetta on the part of ...."

"On the part of who?"

"I'm not quite sure. The German police? No, I don't think so. The Stasi? No surely not but he hinted that he'd had a bad experience in Germany. Enraged lover? I really don't know."

"But didn't he say?"

"Well he sort of did and he sort of didn't..."

I knew exactly what she meant.

When, later, in bed, we returned to the subject, "Think it's true?" I said, stirring Claire up with my elbow. "Think it's true?"

"As a matter of fact, I don't. Something may have happened in Germany and I suppose something did, but this cloak and dagger scenario that he's built round himself, I think he's done it to make himself feel important and it came to me while he was talking that if I were to prove that it was all nonsense, the props that sustain him would have been knocked away. Perhaps you should go along with it?"

"Know what you mean. I knew a guy with a heart condition. Couldn't do this, couldn't do that. Everyone was sorry for him. Congratulated him if he occasionally got off his arse. What happened? Suddenly his doctor changed; suddenly he hadn't got a heart condition - misdiagnosed years ago. He was just like everybody else. He couldn't bear it. Went to pieces completely. Chris Parry could be a bit like that I suppose."

"Yes, rub out his defining ailment and what have you got left? Look Jack, kicking away props, removing a protective shell - that's dangerous stuff and it's not up to us. I don't think we should meddle with this. Could you get Christopher to see a psychiatrist do you suppose?"

"I'll try," I said despondently, "but I don't think it will do any good."

And for that night, that was where we left it but I continued to puzzle and to worry about Christopher Parry - whether he was genuinely in trouble in which case he needed some help or whether he'd made the whole thing up, in which case he needed some help. I tried to put this to him one day when we were alone in the office.

With a return of his normal manner, supercilious, disdainful and deeply suspicious, he eyed me in frozen silence for a moment or two and said at last, "I didn't think it would be long!"

"What do you mean?"

"I didn't think you'd hold out long," he said and stalked from the room.

A very few days later, a few days in which he'd got in even earlier and stayed even later than usual, he stalked from the office, never to return. No word, no nothing.

I wrote him a letter:-

"Christopher, I'm worried about you. Please stay in touch. Whatever you may suppose, I, we, all of us will help you if you'll let us. Remember this. Yours, Jack."

I worried on, however, but was more concerned at this time with, on the one hand, the collapse of Byam's romance with Gentian and, more cogently, with the problem of how on earth I was going to run the office with a very preoccupied Byam and no Christopher Parry.

It was, though, at this moment that Kirsten dropped from the sky into our laps. In the short term at least, I was never more pleased to see anyone. With a sigh of relief, I handed her Christopher Parry's job which was ready to go out to tender and with exemplary calm, she picked up the reins and drove it forward.

A few weeks later she summoned me to her side. "Jack, come over here and have a look at this," she said without preamble. "Am I mad or is there something quite bizarrely wrong with this drawing?" And she pointed.

In the corner of the pub garden there was a pond. The pond was surrounded by flowering trees. I gazed. One of Parry's best. A perfect drawing. "What's the matter with that?" I asked.

"Look again more carefully," said Kirsten. "Do you see what's going on under the trees?"

I looked again and, if you can believe, meticulously drawn and absolutely unmistakable, under each tree was a little figure seen from above, more precisely a little male figure and more precisely yet all were peeing in the pond. There were other things besides. A little note on the drawing said, 'Reception Hall'. It had been changed to 'Reception Hell'. On the floor above 'Double Bedroom' had been changed to 'Trouble Bedroom'. There were four wcs in the ladies' lavatory and neatly drawn on each of these there was a seated figure and the words, 'Simpson, Alexander, Steel and Munro'. There were two rats in the kitchen and what was, I believe, meant to be a cockroach on the bar counter.

"He was a funny man, your Mr. Parry," said Kirsten.

"I'll say he was a funny bloody man! Well, I suppose we'd better scratch these things out. Oh, and Kirsten, have a really good look and make sure you've found them all. How many copies of this drawing have been issued?"

"None yet," said Kirsten. "I was just going to do it."

Later she reported thirty Parry jokes, some harmless, one or two very rude.

And so the job started and was set out on site.

Dimensions on drawings are of two sorts. There are the long dimensions, that is to say a single dimension which delineates - as it were - one side of a building. This might be, for example, 17.50 metres. There are also the short dimensions and these divide the long dimensions into sections indicating the size of the windows, the door openings, projecting piers and so forth. Obviously, the sum of the short dimensions should - and indeed must - equal the long dimension. The job was well started on site before Kirsten who was just packing up at the end of the day received a panic-stricken telephone call from the site.

"Something seriously wrong here!" said a voice. "We can't make head or tail of the dimensions. Here... have a look at drawing number 15 for example. You have a long dimension of 15 metres but the sum of the short dimensions is 17! I can't make it out! It doesn't scale. We've got half set out on site. Bit of a problem? You can say that again! The guy who drew this must have been pissed out of his brains. I suppose it wasn't you? I've called the blokes off for today. Do you think you can get over here first thing tomorrow?"

Kirsten brought this problem to me and we looked at the drawing in question. It was all too horribly true. From the chest we extracted an earlier copy of the drawing. On this, dimensions both short and long added neatly to the same sum. We looked again at the negative. There was no doubt about it - Christopher Parry had altered every dimension on every drawing and we had issued six copies each of thirty five drawings! We looked at each other in consternation. At least I looked at Kirsten in consternation. She looked back at me with competent calm. "Leave it to me," she said, taking off her jacket and rolling up her sleeves.

In due course, much to the amusement of everyone else concerned, we sorted the problem out, we issued the corrected drawings, we heaved a deep sigh of relief and cursed Christopher Parry. I remembered his words, "Nobody tangles with me and gets away with it!" Had I tangled with him? I didn't think so. But there we were.

There was, however, a measure of light relief at the end of this rather dark night. Byam took a call from the

Goldhawke Design and Build Partnership. Having announced himself, the oily Mr. Goldhawke proceeded,

"How's business in Lavenham? Plenty to do? No hard feelings about the shopping mall I hope? Some we win, I always say. Ha, ha, ha. But that wasn't what I was ringing up about. We've just had a job application from a Mr. Christopher Parry. Anything known? We gathered indirectly that he'd been working for you recently."

Byam drew a deep breath. "Christopher Parry?" he said. "Ah yes. Charming chap! Good architect. Pity he left us when he did - personal reasons I believe. Oh yes, I think you'll do very well with Parry. I wouldn't hesitate if I were you. Tell you what - why don't you put him onto the shopping mall? It would be just his sort of thing..."

"That's just what we were planning," said Mr. Goldhawke, gratified.

"You couldn't do better," said Byam.

III

A Dishonest Crust.

In the architectural profession jobs can become totally absorbing. Clients can become totally absorbing too. In the hothouse of a building project friendships blossom overnight. You find yourself after six months talking to a client practically every day, a client who six months before was completely unknown. An unfamiliar journey becomes a wearisome and totally familiar journey. The preoccupations of a complete stranger become your own. In the context of domestic work you find out surprising things about your employer and so it goes on but, a year - two years - later, and suddenly it is as though they had never been. You forget the details of the job, you forget your client's christian name, you even forget how to find the site. It is really very strange. I suppose the same thing happens at the other end; the architect - once a household name, a name on every lip, the subject of alternate love and hate, the recipient of acid memoranda, the recipient of occasional grateful thanks - fades into the past and is forgotten.

I sometimes observe the rolls of dusty drawings in the attic at Spring House, some thin, some thick, (some even enormous) and contemplate with wonder verging on dismay the hours of forgotten toil which these records represent. Sir Hastings had been in practice for forty five years; at the rate of - say - twenty jobs a year that represents

21

nine hundred jobs more or less, nine hundred blood-curdling crises, nine hundred sleepless nights, nine hundred forgotten friendships. The mere idea leaves you feeling tired.

Amongst these dusty cylinders - canopic jars containing the débris of creation - there was a particularly thick series of rolls. 'The Mecklenburg Club'. Thirty years ago it must have formed an important part of Hastings' life but no more. I knew nothing of the Mecklenburg Club save that, as such, it had ceased to exist. As with so many other London clubs it had merged with a like-minded establishment and there was really no reason in the world why the drawings should not be consigned to the skip and the serried ranks of associated box files likewise. I even pulled one out with this vague intention when the telephone rang. Summoned by Heather, I hurried downstairs and was unable to believe that such a coincidence could be when a bland voice - with a touch of London's east end I thought - spoke to me.

"I understand your firm were responsible for the alterations and improvements at the Mecklenburg Club. Am I right or am I wrong?"

I told him he was right but added deferentially that it was before my time. He didn't seem particularly interested in this information and went on without a break saying accusingly, "I've had quite a job locating you. The only address I had for your firm was in Gower Street."

I said that Sir Hastings had left Gower Street thirty years before and the voice continued, "Well I'm coming to you because you've got the drawings and I'm always anxious to cut costs and cut corners and I don't want to lay out a lot of money on an expensive survey. You seem to be the only people with any records... I assume you still have the records?"

I reassured him on this point and he went on, "I'm keen to save time so I'd better come down and see you. Three o'clock this afternoon be all right?"

22

As it happened three o'clock that afternoon would have been fine but I didn't want to seem eager so in a cautious and temporising sort of voice I said, "Um, well, three thirty would be better... Can you tell me what this is about? And can you tell me who is speaking?"

Impatiently the reply came back, "I'll tell you all about it this afternoon. Three thirty." And he rang off.

"That was a funny one," I said as I went to give an account of this strange conversation to Ron. "Don't even know who he was. He didn't leave a name, didn't leave a telephone number."

"Doesn't sound like anything much to me," said Ron. "Probably wants you to re-washer a tap on the third floor."

I agreed. "Probably," I said.

Ron, of course, knew all about the job and helped me to carry down the drawings which had been put away in no sort of order, which were crackling with age and so tightly rolled as to be as easy to read as a steel spring and very dirty from having spent thirty years in the attic at Spring House. It took us some time to sort out an appropriate set to present to our visitor. We assembled floor plans and after searching through a second roll of drawings, elevations. Heather fed these gently through the dye-line copier and in the end we had a crisp and efficient collection of drawings to present to our visitor.

"Nice house," I said. It was a nice house. Early eighteenth century, stone-built, both discreet and pretentious, it was quite a building. "Listed Grade I, I should think," I said, my interest beginning to warm.

"Bad roof," said Ron. "Badly designed roof, that is. Had a lot of trouble. Look at this..." His finger traced the wandering course of a valley gutter which, it seemed, ultimately discharged through a single internal rainwater pipe. "Whole blooming issue discharged into an underground catch pit," said Ron. "Fresh water well, you know the sort of thing."

Having laid out our selection from the dusty memorabilia, I went to seek out Kirsten. "Are you in at three thirty?" I said. "Come and back me up. Want to put on a show."

In a voice characteristically void of enthusiasm and saying, "Can give you half an hour, can't spare more. Got to get this thing finished today," she agreed to show the flag.

At three twenty nine a large black Rolls Royce with up to the minute (it being the third of August) number plates came stealing down the street. The driver with his window down was peering at house fronts as he came and finally parked on the cobbles in front of the house. I shouted to Kirsten, "Come and look at our client! Posh stuff, eh?"

I looked her up and down. Tee shirt and jeans. I looked myself up and down. Tee shirt and jeans. "Just run home Kirsten and change, will you?"

She didn't think this was funny but then she didn't often think my jokes were particularly funny. "He won't notice what you're wearing," she said repressively.

Heather showed our client in. He was the neatest man I think I have ever seen. The whitest shirt, the most unnaturally shining shoes, the darkest grey suit, the silkiest tie, the most discreet gold cufflinks and the most expensive Swiss watch. He was small and slim. He had very small hands and feet. His spectacles were gold rimmed. He was dusky of complexion and lustrous of eye. His name was Everard McBride. He was, he told us, the Managing Director of the McBride Group. The McBride Group were multiple tailors - if you can have such a thing as multiple tailors and definitely upmarket. I fought down a naive urge to confide that my wedding suit bore the McBride label and restricted my response to an understanding smile and a nervous tug at my jeans.

Our new client spared little more than a glance for the drawings and at once unfolded his own plans which were to convert the Mecklenburg Club into a prestige headquarters office for the McBride Group.

"Now I want you to be a sport," he said almost without preamble. "We're going to have a battle on our hands with the planners. If we're going to maximise the potential, we shall need another storey. You can do that in one of two ways. You can add a storey - and I think the planners would wear it - or we can rip out the entire interior and rebuild behind the façade and that's where I want you to be a sport. I said I was coming to you because you had the drawings but that's not the only reason. I'm coming to you because I understand you have a certain reputation with old properties. I want you to say that as it stands it's beyond repair."

Kirsten and I gasped a bit.

"Is it beyond repair?" asked Kirsten suspiciously.

Everard seemed to notice her for the first time and, not having had an opportunity to do so before, I introduced her, "My colleague, Kirsten Munro."

He didn't take very much notice, merely saying, "If it isn't beyond repair it soon will be."

We discussed the matter a little further. He produced a typed schedule of accommodation. Poring over the drawings, he released a flood of information. "Boardroom here, my office, my PA's office, food-preparation unit, banqueting room, reception here, three floors of general offices, bathrooms, toilets, private entrance from the mews..." He rolled on.

It came to me that if this was a true bill it was a very big job indeed. I thought it extremely unlikely that the planning authority would agree to gutting the whole thing and starting again and I wasn't absolutely certain that I could be a party to so nefarious an act though I was mindful of Ron's observations in the matter of rainwater disposal and wondered whether there could be an absolutely life-destroying outbreak of dry rot as McBride seemed to think.

At the conclusion of this meeting, during the course of which our client had let two cups of coffee go cold untouched, he set off back to London with a roll of prints under his arm and leaving me with an appointment to visit the Mecklenburg Club, now to be called Mecklenburg House, early the following week.

Kirsten and I settled to contemplate each other.

"Didn't like him," said Kirsten. "Twister if ever I saw one! Tell him to go somewhere else. You'll regret it if you don't."

For a second the awful thought that she might be right flashed through my mind but I decided to ignore it. It was a very substantial job.

It was a very substantial house, as I was to find the following week. Dusty and neglected, it had been empty for ten years and still with sorrowful evidences of its happy hundred and fifty years as a smart club, soon, presumably, to be swept away. Rooms - rooms, that is on the ground and first floor - were lofty and ornate, decorated to the least possible advantage in sage green and brown. I would guess that the paint had been applied at least fifty years before. Cavernous basements enclosed wine cellars and kitchens. Bare patches on the walls recorded the positions of mighty portraits, now dispersed. The place was decorated with little notices - 'Gentlemen are requested to do this', 'Gentlemen are particularly requested not to do do that,' 'Gentlemen wishing their mail to be held are to notify the porter.'

It was solid, it was comfortable, it was elegant, it had a great deal of ponderous charm. I liked it. I didn't like what we were about to set out to do.

I had first to disabuse Everard of any suggestion that the structural condition was such that it would justify any wholesale destruction of the interior. He eyed me with sly complicity, saying, "You'd better come and see," and he led me upwards and upwards and finally through a breakneck attic stair onto the roof. Large sections of lead had recently been hacked away, the single rainwater pipe had had a bundle of old sacking stuffed into it. One or two slates were broken, a roof light stood open.

"Vandals!" I said. "When did this all happen?"

"Last week," he said.

"Last week? How do you mean - last week?"

"Now, come on, Jack!" he said. (We had swiftly advanced to first name terms.) "Come on Jack, think a bit! You've got to do what you can to encourage the process of collapse. Leave it like this for six months and we'll have a dry rot outbreak from attic to basement! I know these old properties. Won't take long to get it going and look here..." He produced from his briefcase a screw-topped jar which seemed to be full of reddish powder.

"Know what this is?"

I knew. "Dry rot spores."

"Right! I've been scattering them around the house for weeks! Lift up a floorboard and shake a few into the floor... pull out a piece of skirting and shove some in behind it... Water coming in through the roof - oh no, it won't be long! Then we'll all say, 'Oh, what a shame!' But by then it'll be too far gone, not worth preserving and then they won't be able to stop me putting another floor in. You've got to be a bit street-wise these days, you know! No good just letting them roll right over you. You've got to take the initiative... preemptive strike, that's the thing. Only thing that works in business."

My hair stood on end. "Everard," I said, "you can't do this! There'd be the most terrible scandal if they caught you at it! You're never going to get consent to rebuild the interior, it's far too important. And, besides, what happens to the staircase if you put a new floor in?"

The staircase was a fine cantilevered stone structure, a wrought-iron handrail of dazzling expertise and complexity following it up the house.

"You'll never get permission to rebuild that, I'm sure of it. In fact, Everard, let me tell you straight - forget it!"

He turned on me, his face expressionless with astonish-

27

ment. "Forget it!!! I can't forget it!! We've just exchanged contracts! What do you mean - forget it?"

Embarrassed, but sure of my ground, I said, "Forget any intention totally to remodel the interior. No one's going to agree to that. And if there's no other consideration, the architect of this pile was James Pomfret and this is the only building left in London attributed to him. The Pitt Club and the Wellington were both bombed out in the war."

"Bombed out in the war? And what happened to them?"

"Well one's where the offices of Equity Insurance are now and the other is the site of Conglomerate House, Picadilly."

"Well there you are. No one said they'd got to be identically reinstated. This is just the same."

"No, Everard," I said firmly, "it isn't just the same."

A spot of angry colour appeared on each cheek. "I was very glad," he said, "to give you your chance. If you don't want it I'll find somebody who does."

"Find who you please," I replied with spirit, "they won't tell you any differently from me."

"I don't usually employ a provincial architect," he said, "and I shall know better another time. I shall go to Chartermarque."

Chartermarque are a powerful firm of commercial architects so grand that I did wonder whether they would condescend to this job but I said, "You're welcome to Chartermarque if that's what you want."

"That is what I want," he said. "I'm sorry you've wasted my time!" and he flounced ('flounced' is the only word for it) down the stairs.

And that seemed to be that. I made my way back to Spring House and told what had happened to loud applause from Kirsten, to understanding sympathy from Hastings, to hearty laughter from Ron and to regret - guilty regret, but regret all the same - from Byam.

"Shame, though, to pass up a job of that size," he said.

"We're only here to earn an honest crust after all."

"This would have been a very dishonest crust," said Kirsten crushingly.

It was not, however, the end of Everard McBride. Six months later, I had just completed the long postponed task of returning the drawings to the attic when he rang up.

"That you old chap?" he asked.

"Simpson, here," I said coldly.

"Everard here. Mecklenburg House. Remember? Well listen. I had to get rid of Chartermarque. Why? Because they're no bloody good, that's why! Wasted my time. Prepared sheet after sheet of drawings with what result? Planning and Listed Building consent refused. But I never mind when people tell me the truth. It's only when they try to lead me up the garden path that I get my rag out and what I admire is the way you gave it to me straight from the shoulder."

"Did I?" I asked, bemused.

"Yes, of course you did. 'Never get planning consent,' your very words and that's how it's turned out six months later. And if Messrs. Chartermarque think I'm going to pay their exorbitant fee they're on the wrong ship! The question is - when can you get on with it? After all this wasted time we're in a hurry. Have to be up and trading in a year's time at the latest. I say - when can you get on with it?"

"Well, er, Everard," I began and he cut in,

"Oh come on, be a sport! Very few alterations internally... not doing much more than installing engineering services and decorating the place. Rebuilding the staircase, of course..."

"Rebuilding the staircase?" I said. "They'll never let you do that."

"They'll have to," he said. "Can't have a building of that size without a staircase."

"How do you mean 'without a staircase'? It's got a

perfectly good staircase."

"Not any more. I knocked it out. Chartermarque ought to have advised me not to but they didn't and now we've got to rebuild an expensive eighteenth century staircase exactly as it was before. They'll find that's a not inconsiderable item in the action for negligence I'm bringing against them."

And so, and not quite sure that we were doing the right thing, we took the job on. I did all the p.r. and attended all the endless meetings with Everard. Ron and Kirsten, working in considerable harmony got out the production drawings. The planning authority, so pleased were they to have frustrated Everard's devilish plans, couldn't agree more cordially with everything we proposed.

The more closely I worked with him, the more surprising I found Everard to be. It seemed at times that he hated mankind and he was sure that mankind hated him. All mankind, that is, except me. I could do no wrong and he never forgot that I'd once given him unpalatable advice and been right. To my acute embarrassment on more than one occasion he introduced me to colleagues as 'a man who'd lose a big contract sooner than give bad advice. Not many like that nowadays!'

Early in the proceedings he invited me out to lunch. I thought a business lunch with the managing director of the McBride Group might be quite an occasion and was thinking, "I'll start with whitebait then perhaps a fillet steak and top it up with île flottante. Bottle of Hermitage? Why not!" Alas - delusive hope - he led me swiftly across several roads and round several corners and up to the restaurant floor of a department store where he ordered shepherd's pie, jam roly poly, a roll and butter and a cup of tea.

"Mother used to bring me here for my birthday treat and I thought, 'One day I'll come here every day,' - and I do," he said with satisfaction, "and I always have the same menu. Find something you like - why change?" The first of many such lunches. It never crossed his mind that I wouldn't have the same.

Embarrassingly flattering though he was to me, he was a pig to everyone else and in particular he was a pig to his unfortunate personal assistant, Wilfred Knightly. In some way I didn't quite understand, 'Wilfie' as he was always called was an elderly relative of Everard's. "Wilfie's getting hopeless," he would say in his hearing. "I mean - look at him! Not good for the company image are you Wilfie? Get a new suit and get that one pressed before Monday." And to me, "He'll have to go, Jack - he'll have to go."

Wilfie listened abjectly to this and other such outbursts, smiling nervously, scuttling mouselike from the room when Everard's onslaughts died away. How anyone could put up with this was more than I could imagine. "Don't let him get away with it Wilf," I said once after a particularly galling display. "He'd never manage without you. I bet you know where the bodies are buried." But Wilf was too abject to react beyond a secret but hunted smile.

"You'll end up in bed with that bloody Everard," said Byam, a spice of envy in his voice. "He even had the cheek over the telephone the other day when I picked it up to tell me you were wonderful!"

"I am," I said.

"I soon put him right," said Byam.

IV

A Dishonest Crust (part 2).

"You know, he's a really crazy man," said Kirsten one day. "I think we may have another Chris Parry on our hands. He suffers from the delusion that everyone's out to get him."

"It's no delusion," I grumbled.

And so it seemed as, one by one, Everard McBride quarrelled with everybody else involved with the job. He sacked the quantity surveyor, he sacked the consultant engineer, he sacked the decorating consultant and he sacked the heating engineer three times. But through the thud of falling heads - living, I was quite sure, dangerously - I managed to keep my footing on the blood-soaked scaffold.

He nominated a contractor of whom I had never heard but he seemed competent enough and the intention was to negotiate a price. At the very last minute he got he sack too and we were out to tender. Characteristically, Everard insisted that the tenders should be opened in his office at twelve noon.

Funny sort of meeting. Just as Everard had settled down with a pile of pink envelopes in front of him, the door opened and there entered probably the most repulsive youth I have ever seen in my life, aged, I suppose, about ten, in the archaic uniform of a fabulously expensive south coast prep school.

At once, Everard's face dissolved into imbecility.

"My son," he said in strangled tones. "This is my son. Come to Daddy," he added.

Reluctantly the youth shuffled towards him and Everard kissed him a very large number of times, a process through which he stood ox-like and unreactive.

"Daddy's busy," cooed Everard. "Daddy's busy for a few minutes, then we'll go out to lunch. You'll like that, won't you?"

No reaction.

Turning to the much-enduring Wilfred Knightly, he extracted, as far as I could count them - about a hundred pounds from his wallet and handed it to him, saying, "Take him out and buy him some things."

Wilf, his face a mask of servile hatred, ushered out of the room young Benjamin McBride whose sulky features were now hideously enlivened by greed.

"Bye Bye, Benny!" said Everard, waving. "Come back to Daddy soon, all right?"

And we returned to the pile of pink envelopes. The forecast of costs was four hundred thousand pounds and the lowest tender received was four hundred and thirty thousand pounds or thereabouts. Wrong by ten percent. Not bad in all the circumstances and I opened my mouth to say so. Everard turned on the quantity surveyor, all trace of drooling paternity wiped from his face.

"Are you going to tell me," he asked venomously, "just how the hell that happened?"

"We haven't checked the figures yet and anyway thirty thousand in four hundred thousand's not bad," said the quantity surveyor defensively.

"Not bad?" Everard shrieked. "You say a thirty thousand pound error isn't bad? Have you got thirty thousand to spare?"

He smartly turned to me. "Do you think thirty thousand's neither here nor there?" And back to the quantity surveyor, "Well, I'm glad you think so because I think like enough that's what it will cost you by the time we're finished!"

The quantity surveyor himself was quite a tough and, unlike almost everybody else concerned with this project was not in the slightest awe of Everard McBride and in seconds a furious row broke out. Fists were shaken, tables were thumped, papers were scattered and the quantity surveyor stormed out.

"And don't have the cheek to send me a bill!" Everard yelled after him as he disappeared.

White-faced, he collapsed in a chair, his hand theatrically pressed to his heart. "My pills," he whispered. "The left hand drawer... my pills and a glass of water..."

And so he remained in a seeming state of syncope while I hovered solicitously, not quite knowing what to say or do. Should I loosen his tie? Should I dash a glass of water in his face? Should I ring for a doctor? I did none of these things for at that moment his loathsome son reentered the room accompanied by Wilf, burdened with bags from Hamleys and one of the largest boxes of chocolates I have ever seen. His reappearance dragged Everard back from the brink of the grave and, with the briefest apology to us, they set off to lunch.

"Can we go to the Mirabelle, Dad?" I heard and,

"Anywhere you like, Son."

"Come with me, Wilf," I said. "I'll take you out to lunch. Shepherd's pie and jam roly poly do you? Cup of tea? Roll and butter perhaps?"

After this unpromising beginning a contract was signed and the job started on site. Sometimes Everard attended site meetings but more often, mercifully, he did not. In his absence, these went smoothly indeed and it swiftly became apparent that Ron and Kirsten had between them hacked together a matchless set of drawings.

When Everard was present chaos reigned. He

interrupted and contradicted. Many of the principals of the firms involved turned up for safety's sake with an assistant and Everard formed the habit of rounding on these unfortunate juniors and subjecting them to a battery of often irrelevant questions.

"What colour are the baffles on the ventilating system in room 23?"

"Er... white."

"White? What do you mean - 'white'? Are they off-white, are they pure white, are they light cream? What do you mean by white? See that I have samples on my desk tomorrow morning. I'm going out at nine - see I have them before that!"

Sometimes Kirsten came with me and in the early days Everard tried this on with her. In the matter of colour -

"Gustavian grey?" he said derisively. "What sort of colour's that supposed to be? Gustavian grey! Huh!"

Kirsten was undaunted. "It's that pale bluish-grey favoured by the eighteenth century Swedish king Gustavus. Number 54032/G/60 on the shade card."

"Have I approved it? Has anyone approved it?"

"Yes," said Kirsten, "you approved it last Tuesday, together with the whole of the folder of decorative finishes. You initialled a copy for us... would you like to see it? Of course, you're at liberty to change it if you want to... there's lots of greys... we could go to a gannet, a gullswing, a gravestone, a grisâtre, a...."

"All right, all right, we'll stay with the original choice but I shall want to see a sample," said Everard, by now somewhat defensive.

"You don't want to see a sample, Mr. McBride," said Kirsten firmly. "You're only saying that to be difficult." And, turning to the rest of the meeting, "Isn't he?"

Everybody looked nervously down at their papers and waited for the blood-curdling scream which usually preceded Everard's dismissal of yet another player.

But no blood-curdling scream came and, amazingly,

Everard learned not to try it on with Kirsten and everybody else learned the same. I was proud of her.

Within seven months the contract reached completion, a fortnight under the contract time and we embarked on what is known as the 'snagging list', that is a list of all outstanding matters, all complaints, all defects in workmanship or materials. Everard was a busy man but this was his favourite part of any building contract. He loved it.

"Look here - here where I'm pointing. Unfinished. That's terrible!"

I knew better by now than to pretend I knew what he was talking about. "Sorry, Everard," I said, "I'm not quite sure what you're pointing at."

"Here! Under here! They haven't painted under the bottom edge of this cupboard door. Thoroughly sloppy!"

And so it went on until one day he summoned me. "There's a yellow stain on the wall of the staircase," he said indignantly over the telephone. "You'd better come and look at it. It's getting worse."

In company with the foreman painter I duly inspected the yellow stain. He was right; there was a yellow stain. We were baffled.

"Something in the plaster mix?" said the foreman painter. "I don't think so. It's as though it were leaching through from the back. And he's right, it is spreading. Oh, what a bugger! Wouldn't it happen on this job! What shall I do? Slap on a coat of flat paint and hope for the best?"

I sniffed. A recently finished contract is a medley of smells, the sealer, the polish, the grout, the paint itself, the detergent used to wash down the stairs. There was a potent blend here but through it all came a smell that I was, in disbelief, able to identify.

With grim foreboding I said, "Get a little plaster off the wall."

We did and we sniffed. No doubt about it. Familiar from

so many crumbling country properties, familiar from my very earliest days - dry rot! Maerulius Lacrimans himself.

"Now just how the hell did that get there?" said the foreman painter, "Miles from any water. No timber anywhere within range..."

"There is, you know," I said. "The whole bloody wall's full of bond timbers. In the good old eighteenth century way you'll find them at about two foot centres vertically all through this wall."

"But dry rot?" he said. "How the hell did that start?"

I knew but I wasn't going to tell. This was the fruit - the belated fruit - of Everard's nefarious attempt to put the building beyond repair. It had lurked. It had waited. The dry rot spores had rested inert. We had just turned the heating on. It was enough. I remembered seeing Everard shaking a little powder down behind a loose piece of skirting on the landing nearby.

Total chaos ensued, chaos so total that I felt bound to call in the omniscient Hastings. In honour bound, I felt I could not let it be generally known that Everard himself had induced this outbreak and we took down parts of the wall, dismantled cupboards, we set the occupation date back by a month, walls were injected, timbers condemned and replaced. The contractor battled valiantly, consoled by the knowledge that he was working on day work rates and couldn't lose.

Everard, surprising man, received the news and its ramifications with icy calm, unsuccessfully bidding for a guarantee but otherwise resigned enough.

After a month, a month in which many fittings had been dismantled and few rooms had not been redecorated, we reckoned that we had dealt with the problem and then there came a telephone call from Everard.

"Now look," he said, "I want you to be a sport."

This formula which had precipitated so many crises sank my heart.

"I want you to be a sport," he continued, "and you must

realise there's nothing personal in this because we've always been pals haven't we, Jack?"

Guardedly I agreed.

"Now the thing is, this is costing me a lot of money and, talking to my solicitors, they tell me there's only one way I can recoup. I know it wasn't your fault but if it came to court it would be your word against mine. Nobody's going to believe a man in my position's going to scatter dry rot all over the building so what I'm going to do is bring an action for negligence against you. Nothing personal, Jack, and I'm sure you realise that, nothing personal at all but you're the only one who's got an insurance cover we can rely on in the circumstances. I want you to be a pal and notify your insurers of a pending claim. I know you'll do that for me and I'll see you're not the loser personally. Okay? Knew you'd agree."

"Steady, Everard, steady," I said. "Hold on a moment. I'm not sure about this..." and would have said more but he cut in rapidly,

"Just wanted to give you an early warning so when the writ arrives on your desk you'll know what it's all about. Your insurance firm will have more sense than to advise you to contest - bound to attract publicity if it went to court and that couldn't be good for you. Knew you'd see it my way and - there - now we know where we all stand. Well, mustn't chat on, I've got to get down to Reading..." And he rang off.

I sat for a while pondering this bizarre proposition and idly wondering why Everard had to get to Reading until I remembered that here was the original emporium of McBride Tailoring and here their head office, soon to be transferred to Mecklenburg House. I supposed he had gone to attend a board meeting, perhaps even to discuss his forthcoming action against us. But, in fact, none of these things. Strange man that he was, Reading were playing at home that evening against Ipswich Town and since his boyhood Everard had never missed a home game.

I tried unsuccessfully to contact Hastings who was abroad and consulted the office as to the tactics we should employ in the matter of Everard's writ. Byam was in favour of quietly passing the whole matter to our insurers but Ron, Kirsten and Heather were full of fight and eager to put all the facts before our solicitors with instructions to contest. Still uncertain, I rang Everard's office and fixed an appointment for three days hence. I was still hopeful that I might be able to talk him out of it. At least I had to try.

Three days later, and not much looking forward to the encounter, I set off to London for my meeting. The minute I entered their offices, it was clear to me that 'something had happened'. I was the target of many an oblique look and where there was usually a drone of ceaseless toil, little knots of gossiping McBride executives were to be seen in every corner of every passage. My announcement that I had come to fulfil an appointment with Mr. McBride was received with meaning looks and I was shown, not to Everard's elegant waiting room, but straight into the squalid, airless and crowded kennel occupied by Wilfred.

Wilfred was a man transformed. Gone was the look of crushed persecution and in its place a figure bursting with glee and pregnant with news.

"Come in Jack," he said loftily. And this in itself was odd as, hitherto, it had always been 'Mr. Simpson'.

"Take a seat," he added expansively, "and I'll get my girl to bring you a cup of coffee."

'My girl'! Since when was the downtrodden Wilfred empowered to beck or call a 'girl'. The foul atmosphere in his room became even denser as he lit a cigar and he leant back in his chair.

"Had a right how d'ye do here in the last few days. Heard anything about it? No? well, we're keeping it under wraps for the moment."

"Wilfred, what can you mean?"

"Ah, well," he said, settling down to enjoy himself, "Everard went down to Reading on Friday, didn't he? And silly born bugger that he is what should he do on the way home - as far as we can make out - but fall asleep at the wheel! There he was, tooling the Roller back to London up the M4 and what happens? He wraps it round a three storey road sign!"

"Good God!" I said. "Is he all right? Was he hurt?"

Wilfred favoured me with a wolfish smile. "Depends what you mean by hurt... Thrown clean through the windscreen - never would wear a belt - picked himself up and walked away from the wreck. As far as we can work it out, he telephoned a taxi on his mobile and came home. Never said a word to anybody. Went to bed as if nothing had happened. And then what? I came in the next morning, half past eight, and went in to see him as per... 'Who the hell are you?' he says. Nothing unusual about that - he has his genial ways - so I laughed a bit."

(I could imagine the scene.)

"He says again, 'Who the hell are you ?' then, 'Get out of my office! Who told you you could come in here?' Well, as I say, I thought it was one of his little games and I don't need to tell you what a pig he can be. But it wasn't only me - it was the same with everybody, and everything! He picks up a file (Commerce Street, Wolverhampton, it was) - 'What's this file doing in here?' he says, 'Bloody job was finished twenty five years ago! Get rid of it.' I tried to explain that it was a current file. 'Don't you tell me how to run my life!' he says, tears the file in half and drops it in the wastepaper basket. Well, it'll give you a bit of an insight into how this firm's run when I tell you that I didn't think very much of it even then and we carried on like this for two or three days and then suddenly the penny dropped! He'd lost his bloody memory!! He didn't know who I was, just about knew who his wife was, remembered where he lived and where the office was and that's about it. Now what do you think about that?"

I was at a loss to tell him what I thought of it. I was hardly able to believe my ears. "So what?" I said. "What now?"

"I really don't know what now but that's not all of it... this morning in the middle of all this, Everard gets up, goes downstairs - no idea where he's going - walks into the road straight underneath a taxi!"

"A taxi! Was he much hurt?"

"Well, enough to put him in hospital and a good job too! Keep him out of mischief for a bit!"

"But what did you do?"

"I rang up Mister George."

"Mister George?"

"Yes, George McBride - Everard's brother. He's a director and a shareholder - they're all shareholders - family company, you know. Everybody around this bloody office has shares in the company except me it seems sometimes. Well, when they'd carted Everard off, of course, I was in rather a strong position," he smirked. "I was the only one who had any idea of Everard's shenanigans and when I wrote them out on a piece of paper for George he nearly had a fit. There were fifteen! fifteen! high court actions pending. Nobody knew anything about them except Everard, and, as far as I could tell George, there wasn't one where McBride's got a leg to stand on."

"So what's happened?"

"They've withdrawn from the whole lot! Including you, if you're interested. Withdrawn! Solicitors called off! God knows what it's cost them! But that's Everard for you! 'The Main Suer' I call him!" He laughed a wheezy laugh.

A bell rang. "Sorry to bring you up here for nothing," said Wilfred condescendingly. "That's Mister George. I'll have to leave you on your Jack Jones, I'm afraid. I expect you can find your way out?" And he swaggered from the room.

I sat in stunned silence. I could only remember infuriating, crooked, mendacious, treacherous, piratical, what very good fun Everard had been. I remembered how he'd always supported me. Above all I remembered so many sticky and companionable jam roly polys. I couldn't bear to think of the toad-like Wilfred able so to expose him to the derision of his brothers, his aunts, his uncles. Acutely, I wanted to be on his side. I remembered how he had thought he had been on my side and how apologetic he had been to find that he had to - simply had to - sink his teeth in my leg - in the nicest possible way.

Disconsolate and puzzled, I made my way to the front office. "Where's Mr. McBride now?" I asked.

"The Lindo Wing, St. Mary's Hospital," I was told and, finding myself passing an Interflora shop, I sent him a large bunch of mixed roses. On a gilt-edged card I wrote, 'With every good wish for a speedy recovery and affectionate regards, from Jack Simpson. (Your architect.)' I found that I meant it.

V

The Romantic Fragment

"Do you," Byam enquired, "want a fortnight's holiday for two in the romantic fragment of a château fort in the unspoiled heart of glamorous Aquitaine? For free? Because if you do I'm able to make you an offer."

I had learned from bitter experience that with Byam there was no such thing as a free lunch. An offer of this nature was likely to have strings attached. I only hesitated to turn it down because a holiday we had arranged had recently and suddenly fallen through. I thought for a bit, weighing the odds.

"What scam are you into now? Timeshare? No thanks - we share quite enough time with you already, mate," I replied ungraciously.

Byam put on his hurt little boy face and said, "No, no! Seriously, Jack, this is an offer you should consider. It comes from Hermione Belton."

Hermione Belton was an old girlfriend of Byam's. Hermione Belton's husband, Clive, had for this reason and that become a faithful client of ours. As a couple they were both quarrelsome and rich. Always with the knowledge that I might be picking up something it would be very difficult to put down, I made an interrogative, though I hoped repressive, noise. Thus encouraged, he pressed on.

"It would appear," he said, "that Clive and Hermione

were driving back from a glamorous and doubtless very expensive holiday on the sun-drenched Côte d'Azur. It would further appear that they had diverted from their route and wandered back through the Dordogne. Passing through Cahors, they were beguiled by an advertisement for a house for sale and on inspection it proved to be 'exactly what I've always wanted - somewhere remote and romantic where we can really get away from everything, darling'. But the point is this:- she wants to buy it (it's quite cheap as far as I can see even for French prices) but Clive wants nothing to do with it, saying sapiently enough, 'I'm not going to buy a ramshackle old heap in France without a structural survey' and I can hear little Hermione's response - 'Oh, Clive, how can you be so mean? It's only 300,000 francs!' and all the rest. It comes down to this - would I be prepared on an all-expenses-paid basis to swap a fortnight's holiday in this mound of rubble for a report on the structural condition? Here's the sale brochure." He passed it across.

'Dating from the 14th century, this fragment of the Château St. Georges in the village of Castel de Quercy a few kilometres east of Cahors, recently restored to the highest standard by a distinguished French architect specialising in the field of mediaeval structure... £300 per week out of season, £500 per week high season.'

And it really did look, from the photograph, very glamorous. It seemed in fact to consist of little more than a round tower with a conical roof with an impressive mediaeval gateway beside it. Small slit windows climbed the tower, large mullioned windows suggested the presence of at least two large rooms. It had:-

On the ground floor: la cave - a wine cellar ('formerly the dungeon').

On the first floor: a spacious lounge with adjoining fitted kitchen. Original 14th century fireplace.

On the floor above: a fine double bedroom with bathroom, shower and toilet en suite.

There was central heating, there was access to a 'rampart roof walk giving a fine panorama over the river Lot', a courtyard garden and there were small local shops nearby in the village. I began to feel tempted. There had to be a snag.

"Why don't you go and do it yourself?" I asked.

"All very well for you," he said. "I know how it would be! Claire would book the tickets, do the packing, deal with insurance and, if I know anything about it, put you in the car and drive you there. Poor old Alexander! Different scene! Lonely, neglected, morose, no one to go with, no one to prepare a steaming bowl of café au lait, to rest me from my labours as I tramp round this doubtless meretricious piece prodding the 'wealth of old beams' with a screwdriver and quacking into a my digital pocket memo speech pad."

"Poor old Alexander," I said. "Surely there's somebody who wouldn't mind going with you for a free holiday? Kirsten!" I said. "Why don't you and Byam go and survey this sinister looking pile?"

Byam cut in. "I've already asked her," he said morosely.

In the rather annoying way she had, Kirsten eyed us both with an austere and dismissive indulgence but, the more I thought of it, the more this seemed rather a good idea. I looked again at the photograph and was again struck by the fairy-tale glamour of the romantic little fragment. I could quite see what a spell it could have cast over little Hermione who probably saw herself en châtelaine, descending its winding turret stairs, keys jangling from her girdle. I remembered that this was a very spectacular part of France and the local wine delicious. It was early spring, too soon for the tourists and, to cap all, we had after all been caught short at the last minute by the cancellation of our long arranged holiday and though I wasn't prepared to tell Byam this, all our papers for France were in order and there had even been little piles of clothes lying about the place for the last few days at the Pottergate to say nothing of a selection of books to read, maps and guide books.

I explained all this to Claire. "What about it?" I said.

"Can't think why you're hesitating! When do we go?"

"Beware! When did Byam ever hand anybody a clean potato? There has to be a snag."

"Now," said Claire, "I see what it must be like for Hermione being married to Clive. Where's the adventurous spirit of the Simpsons, I'd like to know? We're going! The blossom will be out and the magnolias, birds will be singing and all for free. We're going!"

And we were. Binoculars, cameras, hydrometer, measuring tapes and the like were loaded into the suitcase along with shirts, jeans, trainers, jerseys 'to be on the safe side', maps, guide books and so forth and with only slight misgivings we set off for the village of Castel de Quercy followed by the effusive thanks of Hermione and a reluctance on the part of Clive which he made no effort to suppress.

"For God's sake, old boy," he said, drawing me aside and muttering conspiratorially, "shoot it down will you? I don't want a bijou, one-bedroomed castle in Aquitaine thank you very much! I don't know how I got myself talked into it but you know" - heavy sigh - "what Hermione's like! Look Jack, er, if you were to come back with news of a dryrot outbreak, deathwatch beetle, subsidence, imminent motorway, you wouldn't get any complaints from me! So long as we understand each other - all right?"

Honesty forced me to say Clive would do better to get hold of a local surveyor in the neighbourhood of Cahors, somebody who understood the local constructional system and who had experience of the ills that assail the fabric of stone castles in Aquitaine.

Clive laid a knowing finger along the side of his nose. "Not going to do that," he said. "Imagine the situation: there's this architect practising locally, hand in glove with all the local builders and surveyors, sees an innocent

46

Englishman coming... They'd take me to the cleaners! Wouldn't trust them as far as the end of the.. er.. jardin. Besides, what are they going to say when I ring them up and say 'Survey this house for me but slam it,'? After all, they wouldn't know what little Hermione's like and I haven't got the French adequately to explain. No, I want my own bloke out there."

I felt I'd cleared my conscience.

And so we set off. The tunnel, Calais, the Périphérique round Paris, Tours, Poitiers, Limoges (one night en route), Brive, (getting warm) and, eventually, a scruffy little agency in the backstreets of Cahors where we picked up the key, considerably delayed by a notice in the window which said, 'Fermé jusqu'à 16.00' While we waited it began to rain and morosely we sat in the car, Claire reading the green Michelin guide entry for Cahors (two stars). The bold pioneering spirit that had led us so far began to ebb away until finally, a very large lady appeared and opened up the bureau. She listened stony-faced to Claire's carefully prepared overtures and, having inspected our passports and extracted signatures in triplicate from both of us, grudgingly handed over a clanking bunch of keys bearing such legends as 'Portail', 'Cave', 'Etage supérieure'.

"'At the beginning of the Hundred Years War,'" recited Claire as we drove off, "'the English seized all the towns in Quercy and Cahors alone remained impregnable. In 1360 it was ceded to the English but the town, still unconquered, refused to be handed over. The citizens would only hand over the keys at the express command of the King of France, protesting that he was handing them over to a foreign master.' You'd say they'd got a long memory in Cahors, wouldn't you? She really didn't want to give us the keys."

We set off for the village of Castel de Quercy through the thickening rain and gathering dusk. French road signs, usually so excellent, became reticent and the village, when

47

at last we reached it, was not impressive. We drove round and round. "How can you miss a bloody great château fort?" I said, peering up one muddy little lane after another and for the third time we made the circuit of the village until Claire suddenly said,

"Look! There it is! Just like the picture."

And so it was. Frowning and forbidding, it extended no welcoming hand to us. We were tired and hungry and beginning to feel increasingly dispirited. We sat in the car for a while observing a massive flight of entrance steps and a decorated portail. The rampart roof walk was invisible in the rain, the conical roof was but dimly perceived. I pressed the horn.

"What on earth did you do that for?" said Claire indignantly.

"Because it's de rigueur, when you arrive at a castle, to wind your horn.

'Dauntless the slug horn to my lips I set and blew.
Childe Roland to the dark tower came.'"

"Come on, Childe Roland," said Claire firmly. "Action front!"

I unlocked the cellar and peered inside before we mounted the flight of entrance steps. "Plenty of firewood in here," I reported, "and we may be glad of that."

I couldn't quite work out the internal arrangements. There was a door to the cellar at ground level, there was a door at the head of the entrance steps, but thereafter, the vast staircase wound upwards. Staggering under the weight of our large suitcases and a basket of goodies for supper, we followed it and found ourselves in a cavernous, vaulted room.

"Just thought of something," I said. "Don't remember anything in the sales particulars about electricity. Did you pack any candles?"

"No," said Claire, "but I've got a torch. Here."

I shone it round the room, finding, in the end, one of those strange little press-button light switches that they have in France. I duly pressed it and a forty watt bulb, suspended from a very long flex from the vaulted ceiling sprang to life. As an illuminant it was about as useful as a goldfish in a bowl and it did rather make me wonder about the skills of the architect who had made the conversion. Claire meanwhile explored the fitted kitchen and here she found another switch which brought into play the most violent neon tube I have ever seen but at least this gave us enough light to see where we were.

Fine room though. Heavily groined ceiling and the most enormous fireplace beside which somebody had thoughtfully left a box of matches and a box of kindling. "At least we're expected," said Claire. We returned to the mighty staircase and wound our way onwards seeking the bedroom and, rather more cogently, the en suite bathroom with, as promised, en suite toilet facilities. We descended to the piano nobile where I proceeded to light the fire. It was very cold.

"Little Hermione's barmy!" said Claire decisively.

"Well perhaps they saw it on a blazing, sunny day. It's certainly not much fun in the rain. Come on, let's have something to eat."

I returned to the cellar and came back with a load of firewood and, on second thoughts, went back again for a second load of firewood. The fire blazed and filled the cavernous recess. I had never know a fire that drew so well. It was clear to me that my load of firewood was not going to last the night so I returned for a third delivery.

While I had been descending and ascending the staircase, Claire had prepared a picnic. This she put on the floor in front of the fire and I was glad to see with it a bottle of scotch and a litre of Cahors. We found we were sitting close to each other.

"Tell you something, Simpson," said Claire. "Under no consideration am I going to sleep in that horrible room upstairs. I will go there when I have to for sanitary purposes but that's it! Let's assemble a cushion or two, bring the bedclothes downstairs and sleep here in front of the fire and then when we get home we can tell everyone how romantic it was."

The picnic cleared away, we proceeded in convoy to the bathroom. "Bugger modesty," said Claire. "You're not to leave me!" The bed we'd made up in front of the fire wasn't good but it wasn't bad and the place was at least well supplied with cushions and blankets. I made up the fire and, gathered up in each other's arms, we lay down in front of it watching the flames flickering on the ceiling. Sleep didn't seem to be an option.

"I'm cold," said Claire. "I'm going to put some clothes on." She shivered out of bed and returned in a jersey and a pair of my underpants. I did the same and as an afterthought, climbed out once more and found a pair of socks.

"And then when we get home we can tell everyone how romantic it was," I said.

Something approximating to sleep began to possess me. I was woken by Claire. "What's that noise?"

"Noise? I didn't hear a noise."

"Shush! Listen!"

"There you are - no noise."

"There was a noise."

I began to drift once more.

"There! There it is again! There. Surely you can hear it?"

I could. It was a little dribble of tripping sound. It might have been somebody running down the spiral staircase.

"It's upstairs. It's in that bloody awful bedroom!"

"No. Coming down the stairs, surely."

"It's not upstairs, it's not downstairs, it's not outside either... it's in this room. Listen - over there. Where's the torch? There's something in the room."

I shone the torch around the room and found no movement, nothing. Clinging together we dared to attempt to sleep. "Just the timbers expanding or contracting with the change in temperature," I said, trying to find something comforting to say, "or rats, it could be rats. Rats in boots." Neither of us believed me.

We lay in silence hardly daring to move. If we moved we got cold. If we put an arm out from the bedclothes, the temperature, it seemed, was sub zero. The fire blazed within a few feet of us. It was too hot to approach any nearer but all around it was - and was increasingly - glacial.

"I'll swear there's someone on the stairs," said Claire. "Now do listen."

There was a thump, a distinct thump from below and another from half way up the stairs. The noises continued through the night, sometimes a solid if not to say rhythmic thump, sometimes a measured tread across the floor above us, once, I believe, a sigh.

Tense and alarmed, both too hot and too cold, dry and thirsty, we lay on together. "What do you think's happening?" said Claire because by now the sounds had begun to run together. There was a tripping, hammering sound, there was a subterranean jar which at times seemed to shake the foundation of the castle. I blessed the forethought that had led me to lay in a good supply of firewood and I kept the fire alight and, by this, incredibly and at last, we almost fell asleep. I was roused from a fitful and troubled doze some time later by a sharp cry from Claire. I looked down on her sleeping face, illuminated by the firelight and as I did so, I was aware, in the flickering dark shadows, of a darker shape silhouetted against the glow of the fire. Searching and staring, a dim figure was leaning over her, gazing into her face. I shot awake and I shot upright, flinging a protective arm round her and she woke with a start.

"What's the matter?"

"I'm sorry... I thought I saw somebody... I thought I saw somebody looking at you. It's gone now."

"I was dreaming that somebody was looking at me. Oh, Jack, what shall we do?"

"What can we do? I'm not moving from the fire."

"No. Me neither."

There was now a drumming coming up from the cave below, drumming in which there seemed at times to be hushed voices. There was a distant rattle from the floor above.

"There are people all round us," said Claire, "doing things."

And so it seemed.

After the longest night in our memory, dawn came mercifully early and by five o'clock we could see across the room, by half past five we could have seen to read and at a quarter to six, stiff and sleepless, we dared to creep out of bed. Outside the sun was shining and I went and opened a window. The cold of the night had dispersed and we hardly needed the radiant heat from the pile of woodash left behind by our night time fire.

"What are we going to do?" I asked.

"I'll tell you what we're not going to do and that's spend another night in this place. Not another five minutes if we can avoid it. Let's get out of here! It was horrible! Horrible! And, look here, let's say this over to each other because soon we're not going to believe it - there was that noise..."

Carefully we compared our memories of the night over and over again.

"If we don't do this, in a little while we won't remember it and, by the way, are you going to do a structural survey?"

"I've done a structural survey," I said. "I'll write it out. It reads - 'This place is uninhabitable.' That's all you have to say."

"Do you want to have a bath?"

"A bath? What? Do you mean take all my clothes off? No fear! We're getting out of here. We'll take the key back and bugger off."

"Tell you what though," said Claire, " - I'm ravenous! Could you manage an egg and a bacon and all that? I could. Only thing is - we haven't got any milk. Here - you

52

do the packing and I'll do the shopping. I'll go up the street and get some milk. I noticed a little shop in the square. Hang on here and I'll be back as soon as I can."

I bundled our clothes back into our suitcase, I restored the bedclothes to the bedroom, I plumped up the cushions and stood by the window waiting for Claire to return. Restless, because she seemed to have been gone an unnaturally long time, I began for the first time seriously to look round the room. Knowing very little about Quercy military architecture, I had assumed that it was originally a guard room but looking more critically, I saw that it had at some time been both grand and comfortable. There was a spacious window seat. A small archway led to a garderobe built in the thickness of the wall, still with its pierced wooden seat. The fireplace - to which I seriously thought we owed our lives - with its flat stone arch and its fluted jambs was a text book piece in itself. Spandrils contained escutcheons from which a rough hand had hacked the armorial bearings. The chisel marks were still to be seen. The floor was covered with small glazed tiles and, cudgelling my memory, I recalled the vault in the cave supporting this. I began to see it almost as a friendly room in the daylight but as I continued my perambulation around the room and walked back to the fireplace, this momentary impression was obliterated as if a light had been turned out. There was a bad influence in the room, a very nasty influence, an influence which even in the daylight was perceptible and frightening. It was, I discovered, concentrated in front of the fireplace.

I wanted Claire to come back again. I decided to wait for her outside and, taking up the green guide I went to sit on the entrance steps. I read:-

'Only a fragment remains of the Château St. Georges comprising a gatehouse and one of the flanking towers. The château changed hands no fewer than four times during the Hundred Years War, finally resting in the hands of the English until in 1452 and the conclusion of the war it was returned to the French crown.

'Its troubles were not over and it remained a bone of contention throughout the Wars of Religion. As its final humiliation, it was largely burned down during the French Revolution. Many houses in the village are built amongst the ruins of the castle and, indeed, raised from the castle walls.'

As I contemplated these facts Claire returned. She looked rather subdued.

"Do you mind if we don't have the full English breakfast as advertised?" she said. "Why don't you make some coffee and bring it down here? Then perhaps we could drive on a bit and have breakfast at the next town we come to?"

I got ready two mugs of coffee and we sat outside in the sunshine to drink it.

"I had the most illuminating conversation with Madame at the shop," Claire said. "She lives just next door it seems - in fact just through that wall. Her house is part of the remains of the other half of the gatehouse. The first thing she said to me when I told her who we were was, 'How did you sleep?' A question loaded with meaning I thought. I told her. She was not surprised! Apparently they have bumps in the night sometimes and one time they even took the floor up to see if there was anything underneath."

"Was there?" I asked.

"No, evidently not."

"So what's her theory?'

"Well, her theory, which I really don't think works is that we are on a limestone hill and it's honeycombed with caves, you know - caverns measureless to man - we're not that far from Lascaux if you think about it - and after heavy rain, and they've just had some heavy rain, you get funny underground noises, you know, in limestone caves they have things called syphons and I suppose when they fill up with water they might make a gurgle or even a booming noise."

I considered this for a while. "That wasn't it," I said.

"That wasn't the sort of noise we heard."

"No I didn't think so either," said Claire, "but I pretended to be enlightened. It seemed to be the polite thing to do. Anyway, as I was showing such a warm interest in the locality, Madame drew my attention to a little local guidebook. I bought a copy. Here it is - 'Folk Tales of Old Quercy'".

The book was little more than four or five sheets, stapled together and obviously the work of a local historian.

"My French is better than yours, I shall read it as we go," said Claire. "Your turn to drive."

We sat in the car together, my hand on the ignition key. "Are we mad?" I said. "Are we going to regret this? I mean - rent paid in advance for another fortnight?" We looked again at the beguiling façade, its honey-coloured stones growing mellow in the slanting sunshine.

"No," said Claire firmly, "we're not going to regret it half as much as we would regret spending another night in that place. I don't want to become another folk tale of old Quercy - beautiful English girl discovered crazed over the body of her husband, frozen solid with a look of staring horror..."

"Mopping and mowing?" I supplied.

"Certainly - mopping and mowing," she said. "Come on, just drive! I'll read you a folksy tale or two as we go."

And she started, partly in French, partly in English, hardly finishing a sentence in the way people do in skimming through a pamphlet.

"... legend of St. Georges .. bla.. bla.. whose miraculous intervention turned back the tide of Gothic invasion..."

"Didn't know they had Goths in these parts?"

"Oh, yes, and apparently they had something called Visigoths too. It says here that a Visigoth Princess called Brunhilda was horribly put to death in the 6th century. They tied her by the hair to the tail of an unbroken colt and she got smashed to pieces. There's a very choice section here on female heroines and martyrs... Oh, here's good old Eleanor of Aquitaine divorcing Louis the 7th and marrying Henry Plantagenet. Good career move, it would seem. And there's a mention of our château... much fought over for its strategically important position... une succession de crimes jette une ombre sanglante sur l'histoire du château... a succession of crimes throws a blood-stained shadow over the history of the castle..." Her voice tailed away.

I drove on, looking to left and right, trying to remember the map, looking for a promising signpost and, in due course, one appeared. St Cirq Lapopie. "That sounds about right for us," I said. "A town with a name like that deserves a bit of attention."

"Hmm?" said Claire, not taking her eyes from her book.

I turned off the road. A good choice! St. Cirq Lapopie was a magical place. Looking at its shining best in the bright sunshine, a slender dominating tower, a persian carpet of red, brown and grey roof tiles and perhaps best of all, perched on a little terrace like a house martin's nest, a tiny café-restaurant at the top of the town, where tables were just being set out and shutters taken down.

"Oy!" I said. "Wake up! Breakfast time!"

Claire came back to me with a start and we stepped out of the car to a smiling welcome from the patron and took our seats at a little table looking down on the noble sweep of the river Lot many feet below us.

"Tell you something," said Claire as we sat in the sun and listened to the birds and waited for our breakfast, "we certainly walked right into it last night! It's all in here..." She tapped the book of folk stories. "Now where was I? Ah, here we are... 'a succession of crimes throws a bloody shadow over the history of the château...' Do you know that, fleeing from the marauding English men at arms, the daughter of the seneschal - 'a girl distinguished equally for her beauty and her piety' was discovered hiding in an upper room of the castle and ravished by the brutal soldiery. Escaping from her assailants, Geneviève fled down the staircase and sought cover in a lower room. There she was cornered by the soldiers, slipped and fell into the fireplace and died of her terrible injuries. The townspeople came in procession and begged that her body might be returned to them and she was entombed in front of the altar of the church of St. Georges. Well, what do you know about that?"

"Ah, well, that might explain one or two things - the running footsteps on the stairs? That horrible bedroom? And there we were stretched out in front of the fireplace in the very spot where all the action was, I'd guess. It's not surprising we had a night to remember!"

"A night to forget," said Claire. "But I think that's what it was all about, don't you?"

I agreed and at that moment four fat croissants, a generous jar of butter and a pot of homemade greengage jam appeared with a large coffee pot. We stretched out our legs with satisfaction. The shadows had lifted.

"What are we going to do now?"

"Stay in this village of course. Why not? Look," and Claire pointed down into the town where a swinging sign said, 'Auberge du Sombral'. We were practically looking down its chimney stack. "That's the place for us. Let's go and see if they've got a room."

They had.

Early though it was in the season, the hotel was reasonably full, only one of its eight rooms being available but this suited us down to the ground after the exigencies of the night. Laura Ashley print curtains and duvet cover, Laura Ashley wallpaper, matching towels, thick bedside rugs and through a pine doorway a lavish shower. We peeled off the clothes in which we had slept, sampled the shower at length and fell into bed not to wake up until the middle of the afternoon. We were received by the owner when we descended with roguish complicity. Putting our raddled appearance when we first arrived together with the speed with which we jumped into bed, Madame had assumed that we were in the opening days of a steaming affair and for the rest of our stay we were spoiled on this account.

"I'm all for the French," said Claire.

After a week at the Auberge du Sombral, in my case three and in Claire's case two pounds heavier, we reluctantly set off to wander our way home, remembering at almost the last minute to return the keys to the agency.

"You were a long time," said Claire when I emerged from this task.

"Yes, I took advantage of there being a fax machine there to send a message to Clive."

"What did you say?"

I read it out to her. It was very short.

"Structural condition apparently sound but desperately, dangerously and appallingly haunted. Firmly advise you not to touch it."

When we got home there were several messages from Clive asking us to ring without fail and I wondered whether he might think he'd been short-changed by my report. Not a bit of it! He was overjoyed.

"Wonderful! Wonderful! Clever old Jack! I don't know how you thought of it old boy!" he chortled happily. "Should have thought of it myself, I suppose! If there's one thing calculated to scare little Hermione off it's things that go bump in the night!"

VI

Dunkleys.

From a shibboleth-ridden upbringing, Sir Hastings had retained a number of idiosyncrasies, the oddest of which perhaps was related to a changing mode of address, dependent on the social status of those he was addressing. Thus, those whom he considered to be his equals he would call by their surname without prefix. Byam and I, had we at the outset realised this, might have been flattered that he should address us respectively as Alexander and Simpson. Those whom he considered to be his social inferiors he addressed with a prefix 'Mister'. Only those with whom he had been in the army, at school or at the University or close members of his own family graduated to christian names. But the working classes - bricklayers, carpenters, the building trades generally, also rated a christian name. Thus: overheard on the telephone - "Now look here, Tommy..." and, "Yes, of course, John, haven't I always said so?" It was not always obvious whether he was talking to Lord Lowestoft (an old friend of his) or to a foreman painter of his acquaintance. To confuse the picture, all clients, whatever their origin, were addressed without prefix unless, of course, Sir Hastings had - as he frequently did - forgotten their name, in which event they became 'dear boy' or, if he was particularly ashamed at having forgotten their name, even 'dear old boy'. If you understood the system it did contain a sort of lunatic logic as a rule. Not always though and, as will be shown, it could lead to confusion.

He and I were booked to spend a week in Lincolnshire. The purpose of our visit is irrelevant and the commission of which we had gone in pursuit ultimately came to nothing but we had an agreeable few days together touring that mysterious county and admiring, among other things, the Boston Stump. "Where it all started, I suppose," said Sir Hastings gloomily and you didn't have to know him very well to guess that he was referring to the colonisation of North America, an enterprise which, despite the favours he had received from that country, he considered to have been a mistake.

Our absence in Lincolnshire coincided - rare event - with a week's absence from the office on the part of Heather. Groaning and complaining she had set off grimly to visit a married sister in Newcastle who had married beneath her to a feckless husband, with a seemingly extremely successful hotel in that unpromising city. Until very recently Heather had categorically refused to let us take on any temporary help during her absences - "It'll take me longer to get everything sorted out than the time it would save by having anybody in," having been her line through years uncounted so you may figure our astonishment when, out of the blue, she announced and without preamble that she had arranged for Claire to come into the office on a temporary basis while she was away.

"Well, stuff me!" said Ron. "Young Claire may live to a hundred but she'll never top that!"

Sir Hastings had left a note for Heather - forgetting, no doubt, that she too was to be away - saying, "Give Gilbert a ring on Monday. Tell him the scheme is approved and that he is to get on with it exactly as we discussed. That's all you need say. He'll know what you're talking about."

To this was attached in Heather's writing a note to say, "Gilbert Macready, (and a telephone number). Ring him on

Monday." And this Claire duly did.

Gilbert Macready definitely qualified for christian name terms. He had not only been in the Army with Sir Hastings, they had actually been at University together and briefly together had worked in the same architect's office. He came in to see Sir Hastings from time to time but where Sir Hastings was pink, prosperous, plump and spry, Gilbert, although presumably an exact contemporary, was faded, not very well and poor. He was, however, or perhaps more truly, had been, a brilliant perspective artist and had indeed long ago given up the practice of architecture to work in this way for others. He and Sir Hastings had put a lot of noble presentation drawings together in the past and several were framed and hung in the office.

As she was bid, Claire duly rang him on Monday and rang him for a long time, so long indeed, that she was about to give up when a very ancient voice said tentatively, "Hello?" Claire began to feel rather silly. She only had Sir Hastings' laconic instruction to go by and realised at once that she hadn't the faintest idea what she was talking about.

"Oh, Mr. Macready," she began, "this is, er, Hastings Munro's office..."

"Heather?"

"No. My name's Claire. Heather's away in Newcastle.."

"Newcastle, eh? Sister giving trouble again, is she?"

"Yes, I think so... um... Heather's left me a message, or rather Sir Hastings left Heather a message and she passed it on to me. He says - 'It looks as though the scheme is approved and tell Gilbert to get on with it exactly as we planned.'"

There was a long pause at the other end, a pause so long that Claire wondered whether Gilbert Macready had gone away but at last he came back with considerable animation, "Well, I'm damned! Well, well, well! Are you sure? Yes, obviously you're sure or you wouldn't have said so. Good

Lord! Well, bless me! I have to say that I thought this one was absolutely stone dead. You know all about it of course?"

"No, I don't know anything about it. I don't even know what 'it' is."

"Ah... well, it's a scheme that Hastings and I knocked together last year. It's a scheme to restore the park at Dunkleys. Eighteenth century, you know... must have been one of the best in the country till it got messed up by the Victorians and completely laid waste in the war. Got all the records of course. It was never finished but we can work out what it was meant to look like. Hastings thought the new owner - what's his name - Ironbridge - might be tempted to put it together as it might have been if we made it look pretty enough. Never thought there was much in it meself. Plenty of money but a stingy old coot, I understand. Well, though, this is quite a surprise!"

During the course of this speech, Gilbert, who had sounded old to the point of senility, became increasingly animated and to a point where Claire felt bold enough to ask, "Are you pleased?"

"Yes, of course, I'm pleased. At least, I suppose I am. Lovely scheme, though I say it myself but there is a difficulty... at least, damn it there isn't a difficulty but lots of people will tell you there is including my blasted doctor, blast him! Haven't been too well, you know, and that's not to be wondered at because I am dashed old, though you mightn't think so. Ah! There! If only we could order these things... this ought to have cropped up ten years ago, then I could have knocked their eye out! But now... I don't know if I can do it any more..."

"I bet you can," said Claire, encouragingly.

"Sweet of you to put it like that but it's the sitting out of doors sketching, you know. Circulation isn't what it was and my hands get cold."

"You could wear mittens," said Claire helpfully.

"Mittens! I do wear mittens but - look here - tell you

what - give me a day or two to think about it and I'll ring you back. How do you spell 'Claire' by the way? Ah, I see. I thought it might be Clare, like the poet. Well, it's been very nice talking to you Claire. As I say, I'll ring you in a few days."

"I do hope you feel you can do it," said Claire.

"You encourage me," said Gilbert politely.

And it seemed, indeed, that she had, for it was not after a day or two but rather less than an hour when he rang back to say that he had sorted out 'his things' ('haven't done any work for months'), that he had found a little folding stool that he used to use on holiday in France, was provisionally planning to make his way to Dunkleys on the following day and added finally and awkwardly, "Don't tell anybody what I'm doing, will you? There's a good girl. If this got back to my doctor, he'd have me in a straitjacket - you know the sort of thing - 'Don't get cold... don't overwork.' They don't understand a damn thing, do they? Can't do a job like this without getting cold and overworking! That's what it's all about!" He broke into a reedy laugh which ended in a cough and left Claire wondering very much whether she'd done the right thing in encouraging him as she had.

She went off to discuss the matter with Ron who was very surprised at the turn of events.

"Didn't think it was a job at all. I only thought Sir H. had dreamed it up to give Gilbert something to do. It's quite true he's not at all well. Had one heart attack and come to think of it," he continued dubiously, "I'm not altogether sure he is up to it. He's a good old boy though."

And he led Claire through the drawing office to admire some of Gilbert's framed drawings which, in their graceful, old-fashioned way were indeed superb.

"It had never occurred to me that anyone who could produce that standard of work could possibly be still alive," she said.

Still full of doubt, Claire wandered back to Heather's office and as she sat down the telephone rang. It was, of course, Gilbert. Inevitably, he had definitely decided to get on with it, "and bugger the doctors! They don't know everything. And, anyway, the forecast's good. Bit of fresh air and sunshine - do me a power of good. If it's like this tomorrow, I'll spend the day over there." He began to cough and was only able to splutter a goodbye before hanging up.

Claire began to worry. Well into his seventies and very frail, short of money and only perhaps thrashing his fading strength to prove he could still do it and perhaps to earn a life transforming fee. She went to see Ron. "Where is this place?" she asked. "I'm going over there tomorrow to make sure he's all right."

Ron provided her with the guide to Dunkleys which was a glacial-looking late eighteenth century stuccoed pile, seemingly, to judge by the photographs, in the middle of a featureless landscape.

"Sir John Ironbridge is away, that I know," said Ron, "so, apart from the waiter and the porter and the upstairs maid, you and Gilbert should have the place to yourselves."

Armed with some sandwiches, a thermos of coffee, an apple and a bar of chocolate, Claire set off the following day, wondering how, in all the surrounding acres of aridity, she was going to find old Gilbert. No problem, in fact. As she parked her car and walked round to the south side of the house an encumbered figure was walking very slowly up a slight hill towards her. He was wearing a large number of cardigans; he had a scarf tied over his ears and had surmounted this with a beret. There was a sketching stool in his hand and a pad under his arm. It was clearly Gilbert Macready.

He came on towards her, pausing from time to time, breathing heavily and looking at the ground. He looked, it had to be admitted, pitifully old and frail and Claire hurried to meet him, automatically reaching out her hands to relieve him of his burden.

"Mary?" he questioned, looking up in puzzlement.

"No, it's not Mary, it's Claire."

"Ah. Thought for a moment you were Mary Ironbridge."

Claire, although flattered for a moment to have been mistaken for the owner of this substantial pile, was less flattered when later she discovered that Lady Ironbridge was sixty three.

"No," she said, "I'm Claire, Claire Simpson. We spoke on the telephone the other day. I came to see how you were getting on." And, "Have you had any lunch?"

"Lunch?" said Gilbert vaguely. "Well I got it ready, put it in a basket, you know. Now what did I do with it? Well, bless me - it's on the hall table! I'll have to have it for tea, won't I?"

He chuckled wheezily and stood for a moment leaning on his stool.

"I've got coffee and some sandwiches," Claire hastened to say, "Would you..?" And they repaired together to sit in a niche under a shell canopy on the sheltered south side of the house.

"Show you what I've been doing," said Gilbert while Claire poured out cups of coffee and he produced a series of landscape sketches of the park. "Tell you what - I thought I'd make a panorama, showing the park from those beech trees on the right across the lake, taking in that little monticule - they were going to put a little pavilion on top but never did. Hastings and I thought we'd put it in - good idea, don't you think? and then round the corner until I can pick up the cupola on the stable block and then I can sketch in all the planting as it was originally intended. There was going to be a bridge here but they never built that either. I'm going to shove it in too. Going to be a big drawing, you know - four, perhaps even five feet long. Should look good though." And then, ruminatively, "I wonder if I can still do it? A few years ago, I'd have finished the thing by breakfast time. But there - been told I mustn't overdo it."

They sat for a minute or two eating Claire's sandwiches and drinking coffee, Claire watching while, to her amusement, Gilbert ate the apple and the whole of the bar of chocolate until, at last, he said, "Are you in a car? Then you can run me down the drive. There's a bus at three so we should be in good time."

"Bus? Did you come by bus?"

"Yes. Don't run to a car these days. Failed me MOT if you know what I mean but the bus is very convenient... and warm. Drops me just by my door and it's not far to walk up the drive. Oh, no, I go everywhere by bus nowadays. Everywhere! Well, to tell you the truth - I don't go anywhere very much but it's good to be back at work again. Once upon a time, I'd have come back again tomorrow and done a bit more but I think I've got all I need, if you could just run me..."

"Run you! Of course," said Claire. "I'll run you home."

And, with the minimum of expostulation from Gilbert, Claire carried his equipment round the front of the house, installed him in the car and drove him home to a little house in a back street a few miles from Dunkleys.

On arrival, he sat for several minutes in the car, saying seriously, "I hope I can do this. I don't see so well as I used to, that's one of the troubles. I can paint - in many ways I think I'm painting better now than I ever have. (Don't do much though.) I seem, belatedly, to have got the art of leaving out the inessentials. Though perhaps it's laziness!"

He chortled on, reminiscing for a moment or two. Claire carried his traps up the short path to his front door and watched anxiously as he fumbled to find the key hole, wondered for a moment whether she was expected to accept his offer of a cup of tea, decided on the whole that she was and entered his tiny front room from which a steep staircase led, no doubt, to a small front bedroom and an even smaller back bedroom.

"Tell you what you can do while I put the kettle on - you can read this to me. These are my middle distance glasses

- no good for reading small print and I can't find my reading glasses anywhere."

'This' was a long and complicated form from the DHS, saying that possibly Gilbert was entitled to Income Support and even perhaps to Housing Benefit and ending with the suggestion that he should call in to the office.

"Don't want to do that," he said. "Certainly don't want to do it until I've finished the Dunkleys drawings. Don't want to sweat all the way into Cambridge. Cambridge!"

"Tell you what - when you've finished the Dunkleys drawings, I'll drive you into Cambridge. No problem - I often have to go - no, rubbish! - I'd be pleased."

And with this as a half formed plan which Gilbert described as a celebratory treat and having drunk a cup of Gilbert's tea, Claire went on her way, worried and promising to ring within a few days to see how what Gilbert called 'the opus' was progressing.

Though there was plenty to do in the office, following Heather's meticulous instructions, Claire found her thoughts constantly wandering to Gilbert and the Dunkleys drawings and, finally, she gave way to her worries and drove over to see how he was getting on. Having, with an effort, remembered who she was, Gilbert greeted her with considerable warmth.

"So glad to see you," he said. "Come and have a look."

He was sitting on a stool that would not have been out of place in a Victorian merchant bank, working at an ancient antiquarian drawing board not very securely balanced on two tables that had been pushed together but which were not at quite the same height. The floor was covered with pencil shavings, a jam jar full of brushes stood at his elbow, little bits of sketches lay around him but, from this chaos, there began to emerge a magical landscape.

"Good Heavens!" said Claire. "How long did it take you to do this?"

"Now, for goodness' sake, Claire," said Gilbert seriously,

"entre nous, eh?" And, continuing in a whispered aside lest - presumably - his doctor might be overhearing, "Most of last night! Still can do it, you see!"

Claire was entranced. "It's absolutely brilliant!" she said sincerely.

"Yes, isn't it?" said Gilbert. "Brilliant - that's just the word I'd use. It's the quality I try to get - brilliance." And he plunged into the technicalities of the watercolourists's trade. "I'm a funny chap," he said at last. "Some people do a pencil sketch, work it up a bit by slow degrees but I don't do that - I choose a little bit here and a little bit there and finish it. And then, in the end, I put the bits together. See, look... here's the avenue.."

And, indeed, there was the avenue. Evidently high summer. The little trees were heavy with leaf and each cast dense black shadow on the grass.

"It's a hot day," said Claire, considering.

"Ah! If you can see that, it's not going to be such a bad drawing after all."

Claire made him a cup of tea. They chatted for a bit but his mind was not on her; his eyes strayed back to his drawing and every now and then he picked up and moistened a paint brush and dabbed a little detail. It was clear that he wanted to be left to get on. Considerably encouraged, Claire took her leave and as she did so heard him muttering, "I wonder if it would have been better in the winter? 'A southerly wind and a cloudy sky, a hunting morn proclaim.' What?"

After two days, having rung but received no reply, Claire drove over to see Gilbert once more. The front door was not locked, from which she concluded he was at home but there was no answer to her knock. Growing worried and calling as she went, she stepped into the hall to be greeted by the spectacle of Gilbert in a dressing gown, insecurely balanced at the top of the stairs. He looked pleased to see her but he looked very frail and for a moment Claire felt a surge of hatred for Sir Hastings, "Careless, thoughtless old bastard! 'Just tell Gilbert to get on with it...' indeed! Does he ever think about anybody but himself?"

"How are you?" she called.

"Not wonderful. Been overdoing it. Always have; always will. Nothing to worry about. Thought I'd take the day off today. Not that I'm not delighted to see you my dear! Give me a hand and I'll come down."

Step by step he descended the stairs and led her into the small front room where he sat down with obvious relief, resting his elbows on his drawing board. Looking over his shoulder, Claire saw the park at Dunkleys laid out before her on a hot summer's day. The monticule was surmounted by a little pavilion, a classical bridge spanned the isthmus between the two lakes, the sun caught the gilding on the stable cupola, the trees were reflected in the water on a golden, windless day. Claire was stunned and only able at last to say sincerely, "What a lovely day!"

Gilbert coughed and chuckled. "Make the most of it while it lasts - it's going to rain - as you can see," and he waved a hand to circling black scraps in the sunny sky. "See - when rooks fly as high as that, it's a sure sign of rain. But there we are, we've caught the best of the weather and that's the important thing!"

Animation had returned during this short exchange but Claire said, "I think a day off is a jolly good idea. And what about food? Are you okay? Can I do any shopping for you? Tell you what - why don't I whip a few things out of the freezer and drive them over for you later? Can you eat fish? I've got a fish pie..." And, in spite of Gilbert's expostulations, this is what she determined to do and this is what she did.

Worried, on her return, to find Gilbert still in a dressing gown meticulously sketching a few more highlights on the lake which had now grown a fringe of reeds amongst which there stood a stately heron.

"Don't come tomorrow," he said absently. "Come the

next day because by then it will be finished and we'll have a little celebration, eh?. Not much more to do really but I like to spend a day tarting things up - trim the paper off, paint a border round it, put a little inscription together, shove in the date, you know, the usual things. The last day's always fun, I have always found."

"See you the day after tomorrow, then," said Claire. "And next time I'll bring a chicken casserole or a shepherd's pie or something."

Gilbert reached out a clumsy arm, patted her absently and told her she was a sweet girl.

Two days later, with a shepherd's pie and a chocolate cake and, as an afterthought, a bottle of wine, Claire arrived at Gilbert's house to find a car parked outside the door which was standing open. As she struggled up the path with her packages a brisk figure emerged.

"Hello," he said. "Who are you?"

"I'm a friend of Gilbert's, Mr. Macready that is. How is he?"

He looked at her dubiously for a moment. "Are you family?" he asked.

"Well, no." There was a pause.

"You'd better come in."

"Something's wrong, isn't it?" said Claire. "What's happened?"

He led the way into the house and paused for a moment beside Gilbert's drawing which in all its glowing splendour lay neatly signed and titled across the drawing board.

"Stupid old twit!" he said. "Stupid, obstinate old twit! What more could I have said? How long had he been working on this thing for? Do you know? Four days? (Four nights too, probably, if I know anything about him!)"

"How is he?" said Claire in dread.

"There's no point in my not telling you... I'm Doctor Simmonds... look, he died last night or perhaps early this morning. He's dead."

70

"Dead?"

"Yes. Heart."

"And he produced this lovely thing. He finished it."

She looked at it afresh and saw written in the softest pencil in a corner of the drawing with an india rubber placed carefully beside it, she read - "Thanks for everything Claire. I felt like Samson Agonistes till you came by - you know, 'eyeless in Gaza at the mill with slaves,' but not any more. Thanks for a wonderful four days. Wouldn't have done it if it hadn't been for you."

Claire covered her mouth with her hand. "Oh, my God," she said. "Do you think that's true? What have I, what have we, done?"

"Well I don't know. What have you done?"

"Encouraged him. Told him he could do it."

The doctor looked at the drawing, seeming to see it for the first time.

"Well you weren't wrong. I don't know anything about this sort of thing but - isn't this wonderful? I mean even I can see that this is a beautiful - an amazing - thing."

He looked at Claire's stricken face. "Don't reproach yourself. See it in the round. He's been ill for a long time. At the very best I wouldn't have given him more than another six months and that only if he took great care. There are worse ways of spending your last four days than producing a masterpiece. And for sure it is a masterpiece, isn't it?"

"I think so. But oh, dear! If I had the choice, I'd sooner have him than the masterpiece."

As they spoke, an ambulance stole up to the door and two efficient persons of paramedic appearance made their way up the path. On the doctor's instructions they went upstairs.

"What are you going to do?" the doctor asked.

"I don't know. I have no place here. I'd only come to bring him a shepherd's pie..."

Later that afternoon, Sir Hastings and I returned from Lincolnshire. I was surprised not to find Claire in possession of Heather's office. Wondering, I rang 14, the Pottergate to hear Claire's subdued voice.

"Are you back?" she asked superfluously. "And is Hastings with you? Don't ask any questions Jack, just come down here will you? There's something I have to tell you and show you."

Catching a note of undoubted urgency in her voice and able to convey the urgency to Hastings, we set off together down the street, to find Claire sitting on the floor, a panorama drawing laid out in front of her.

"Hello, young Claire," said Hastings cheerfully. "What have you got here?" But then, catching sight of her tearful face, "Oh, hello? What's all this?"

Claire gestured towards the drawing and sat back on her heels.

"What on earth... what on earth's this!"

Sir Hastings went down on his knees. "Good God!" he said. "Who did this?"

"Gilbert, of course."

"Gilbert? But how on earth did this happen?"

"What the hell do you mean, 'how did this happen?'" said Claire angrily. "You told Gilbert 'to get on with it' - he got on with it and, God dammit, it's killed him! Gilbert's dead! Do you realise he worked solidly for four days? He finished the drawing and it killed him. You should never have asked him to do it!"

"Gilbert? But why? Gilbert?"

"Look," said Claire, "you left a note to say tell Gilbert to get on with it so I did."

"Did I?" said Hastings. "By God, yes I did! But I didn't mean Gilbert. I meant Gilbert at Gilbert and Fords - Percy Gilbert, the quantity surveyor. 'Get on with it,' indeed but what I meant was get on with taking off the quantities for that Norfolk job. I didn't mean Gilbert Macready. That's terrible! And Gilbert's dead, you say? I can't believe it!"

Claire explained the events and developments of the last few days and we knelt together in a row and looked at the drawing.

"Bloody old marvel," said Hastings sadly. "One of my oldest friends and now he's dead, you say. What a lesson to me! What a lesson!"

He sat dismayed on the floor and for a moment he looked - what it was so easy to forget, and what was indeed the case, that he was - an old man himself. After a while he collected himself and set off slowly up the street to Spring House leaving Claire in grief from which I was unable to console her.

Later I joined him in his office. There was a faded photograph in front of him. Three young men in the baggy shorts of the eighth army stood in front of a battered armoured car on which was painted the jaunty palm tree of the Afrika Korps. He pointed. "That's me," he said, "that's Gilbert and that's Corporal Macalistair. Alam Halfa, September 1942. We were all smart fellows then. But now? What on earth do I do now?"

I had thought of this. "You get a colour print made and you send it to John Ironbridge. We can't just put it away in a drawer."

"I wasn't going to. I was going to frame it and hang it where I could see it. Remind me not to be such a careless bastard. Gilbert! Poor Gilbert! But, yes, you're right. Send it to Ironbridge. He has, at least, to see it."

A few days later he drove to Dunkleys, panorama in hand and was late returning.

"Well?" I said as he entered the room.

"Well!" he said. "Better than well! He went for it and so did Mary. 'Do it!' he said. Just that - 'Do it!' They couldn't put it down! So there we are. Oh, God, how he'd laugh! Of all the things we ever did together, this, the last, has to be the greatest. Dear old fool that he was! What a triumph!"

VII

Cameron's Kitchen

"What are you doing?" I said to Byam, peering over his shoulder.

"Oh, just a little drawing."

"I'm not quite half witted! I can see it's a little drawing. What I meant to ask was of what are you doing a little drawing?"

"Oh, just a little job."

"And what's your dear little job called? Or, more cogently, who's your dear little client?"

There was a long pause and Byam, finally driven into the open said, "It's a little job for Roderick."

"For Roderick! What's this? The extension to the west wing? Dammit! I was going to do that! You bugger! You knew I was going to do it! You sneaky bastard!"

"Oh, come on, Jack!" said Byam, laying down his pencil. "What does it matter who does the drawing so long as it gets done? When he rang up he seemed to be in quite a hurry and I knew you were up to the balls with Woodhouse's job so I said I knew all about it and that I'd do it. I'm sure you'll be glad to hear that he was extremely grateful."

"Well let me tell you that the next job that comes into the office having even the faintest pretension to being of the slightest interest or requiring even the barest minimum of design input goes to me! OK? Got it?"

"Yes, yes, of course, old mate," said Byam. But I could see that he was so interested in what he was doing that he was hardly taking any notice of me.

Nor was the rest of the morning any more encouraging because I went in to see Heather to be greeted with the words, "Woodhouse has been trying to get you. Here's the number."

'Woodhouse' was the job on which, at that time, I was principally engaged. I noticed with a premonitory flutter of the heart that the number was a London telephone number and not, as customarily was the case, a local one.

"That you, Jack?" he said when I finally got to him. "Thanks for ringing back. I say, look, we had this board meeting yesterday afternoon. God, what a party! Started at two and didn't get up from the table till six! Quarterly figures not wonderful. Nothing like Carter had led us to expect. Anyway, Jack, the long and short of it was the board have decided not to go ahead. I repeat, not to go ahead, at least for this year. 'Review the situation in the spring'. Doesn't look very good, I'm afraid. But Jack, look here, thanks for all that you've done. Much appreciated and, I say, let us have your account will you? See you soon perhaps? Give us a ring. We'll have lunch."

Ron came into the room at this juncture and, after one look at my face (and forty years of mixed experience) he was able accurately to assess the situation. "Woodhouse job gone up the Swannee has it?"

I nodded dumbly.

"I never did trust that Woodhouse," said Heather. "Slimy Woodhouse! Get our account out, shall I?"

"Yes," I said, "and don't spare the horses!"

I really was annoyed about this. It wasn't that we were exactly short of work (there are always loose ends to be tied up) but this Woodhouse débâcle did coincide with one of those slack periods in the office and I didn't believe Woodhouse's explanation. I felt it probable that it was he who had persuaded the board to drop the job for the time being. I looked at my watch. It was twelve o'clock. On an impulse, I decided to go home for lunch and strode wrathfully down to the Pottergate to pour my woes out to Claire.

"Well, I'll tell you exactly what to do in such circumstances," said Claire. "The strong, manly course would be to take the afternoon off. Come on! You haven't for ages. Let's! It's a nice day, let's go and have lunch at the Cockerel and then go and see if Norman and Charles have got anything interesting."

This seemed a very good idea to me. The Cockerel gave a very good lunch of the cold beef - salad - pickled walnut - Adnams ale variety and was a pretty little building in itself. Norman and Charles were antique dealers in the village beyond and Claire, over the months had struck up a considerable friendship with them. Their shop was full of good things, bad things, kitsch things, neat bits of fakery with spray-on cobwebs and carefully drilled wormholes. I even once found Charles dropping a page from a totally irrelevant Victorian letter into a little box on the lid of which he had just carefully painted an only just decipherable inscription and a date which could have been either 1683 or 1883. "That'll give us something to talk about while they're sorting out their cheque book," he had said.

The lunch was satisfactory, the day was fine, the drive had been pretty and Norman and Charles were welcoming, especially when we told them why I had decided to take the afternoon off and were full of clucking sympathy. "What you need, dear, is a nice bright cup of tea. Leave it to Aunty Norman," and he bustled away.

"How much for this Sunderland lustre plate?" asked Claire.

"Twenty pounds, dear," said Charles. "But fifteen to you."

Claire and I took the little plate, which was, indeed, extremely pretty with a ship in full sail in the middle and an inscription round it reading, 'The ship that goes and the storm that blows and the lass that loves a sailor.'

"Norman," said Claire, "it's worth a lot more than fifteen pounds you know." But Norman wasn't listening, for, at that moment, a large figure came heavily into the shop.

His face seemed familiar but, after a moment's scrutiny, I decided that he might have been any one of half a dozen Roman emperors. Tiberius? Nero? And perhaps I had seen him as a bust. Without preamble, he addressed himself to Charles and Norman -

"Ah, shit! After all that goddam work! Ah, Jesus! It looks as if Timperlys is all washed up so hold the Boulle cabinet for the moment!"

"Oh no! But why?" shrilled Norman and Charles in chorus.

"Just had the goddam architect swarming all over the goddam house! It's going to cost another fifty thousand and I just don't have that money in the old jeans pocket! I'll just stick the car round the back and if you've got a little brandy I'll say thank you!" And he swept out of the shop.

"Who was that?" said Claire.

"Lord, darling! You don't know much do you?" said Charles. "Don't you ever watch the telly? Thursday night at eight? 'Cooking with Cameron'? Never seen that face before?"

He flashed a copy of a glossy magazine on which the face of Robert Cameron - much as recently viewed, save that here he was smiling expansively over a large dish on which there appeared to be a covey of roast partridges - was displayed.

"Of course! 'Cameron's Kitchen'! It's on all the book stalls. And hasn't he got a restaurant in London?"

"Yes, dear, that too. But he's been wanting to establish a five star restaurant in Suffolk for ages. Been trying to buy Timperlys. That fabulous house! You must know it! He wants to live there in splendour and state if I know anything about him. It's a very good idea but he just seems to be short of that odd few thousand. Shame, we really thought he'd made it this time..."

"Who's his architect, I wonder?" I asked curiously.

"Tristram Thornton," said Charles with disparaging emphasis. "Don't see the point of him, myself, but Robert thinks the sun shines out of his tiny bum."

"I wouldn't believe a bloody word from Tristram Thornton," I said. "He tried to stitch up some clients of ours and nearly had them underpinning the whole of the back of their house. Luckily, they got a second opinion from Sir Hastings. Absolute balls! Quite unnecessary, the whole operation! But the on dit is that he is pushing three sons through public schools and needs every penny he can lay his hands on. But," I turned to Claire, "we ought to be going. Poor Mr. Cameron wants to sob on the shoulders of Norman and he won't want us around."

"Are you sure fifteen pounds is all right?" asked Claire.

"Give us a kiss dear and you can have it for ten," said Norman. "It's cracked, you know."

"You can have fifteen pounds and a kiss," said Claire.

"That was clever of you," she said to me as we drove away, "what you said to the boys about Tristram thing."

"It wasn't clever, it was true."

"Yes, but it was a clever thing to say! I bet they'll tell Cameron and I'll bet he'll be on the phone almost before you've got home."

As so often the case, she was right and, when we entered the Pottergate the phone was ringing. A rich American voice, instantly recognisable as that of the author, showman, television personality, bon viveur and toque de l'année, Robert Cameron.

"Mr. Simpson? I hope your ears have been burning? Our friends Norman and Charles have been saying nice things about you! Do you want to come and look at a house with me tomorrow morning? At about eleven o'clock? And stay and have a bit of lunch with me? You can? That's fine! Bring that sweet girl with you and we'll all have a look round together. You know the house?

Timperlys?"

I said I didn't know the house, but I knew where it was and thanked him very much. We would both look forward very much to meeting him there at eleven the next day.

"Well, I'm damned!" I said.

Timperlys was almost, if not actually, the most beautiful house in Suffolk. Originally an E shaped Elizabethan house, it had had a most comprehensive 18th Century face lift and the front elevation was neatly rusticated and stuccoed and equipped with an elegant suite of sash windows. An arcade supporting a gallery had embraced and concealed an originally projecting porch. Deeply peaked roofs showed above the parapet dressed out with huge octagonal shafted chimney stacks. The rear elevation was much as its original builders had left it four hundred years before. There was a nettle-grown service courtyard with sagging roofs and crumbling brickwork, leaking gutters and a débris of old boilers, a rusting washing line and the most enormous mangle I have ever seen. The ground floor rooms, dusty and neglected, were in the main, finely panelled. Each contained splendid marble chimney pieces of the early C 18.

Robert Cameron, accompanied throughout the tour by two obese, asthmatic and disdainful pugs, led rapidly from room to room. "I guess this'll have to be the kitchen - shame because it's a good room, but I don't see what else. And this could be a staff sitting room through here and - just look at this! Did you ever see such a pretty little room? I see this panelling dragged in a sort of pale straw colour and we'll keep it for private parties - you know, ten or so. Come and look at this! What about this! Just look at that fire place!"

He opened the shutters. "Jesus! Did you ever see anything like the garden? Hell, wait till next year! I've got a guy coming to talk about it. I want to get that fence out of the way and build a ha-ha and then you'll get a view right down to the church. But here - through here - now this really will knock your eye out!"

He opened another door and we stepped into the saloon which swept upward for two storeys to a painted ceiling. Half a glance told me that a main tie beam had gone. Half a sniff revealed the presence of dry rot.

"There used to be another mirror here, but it fell. I've got photographs to show what it used to look like. We'll get it copied. Now come up this other staircase." And to Claire, "Now just hold my hand and shut your eyes. I don't want you to open them until I tell you. Right, now, look up and open your eyes... now!"

Claire did as she was bid and gasped. There above us with all the exuberant grace and skill of that inspired period was the most wonderfully elaborate Carolean ceiling. Robert, tearing the shutters open and waving his arms, led Claire by the elbow and pointed out its charms to her. "Just look at the little birds in the corner," he said, "and the way the vine leaves follow that circle - medallion would it be? - they say there are four fine ceilings in East Anglia - Felbrigg, Melton Constable, Hintlesham and Timperlys. I guess Timperlys is the finest. I'll keep this room for myself." And to me, "Do you think you could put a bathroom in here? I'll have this as my bathroom and this as my dressing room and," again to Claire, "through here, my bedroom. I've got a fabulous fourposter bed and when I wake up in the morning the sun will be just coming through right there. What do you think? But wait a minute, I was forgetting..."

We returned to the gallery and he opened what I had supposed was a section of panelling but which now revealed itself the door leading to a wide staircase and to the attic storey.

"Ten bedrooms up here," he said. "Didn't even know they were here until Norman told me. Plenty of staff accommodation."

We walked on, opening the door of one dusty room after

another. Unexplained changes in level produced odd little flights of stairs. An elliptical window in the centre of the eighteenth century pediment over the front door filled the beamed and dusty attic with shafts of golden light. The condition of the attic over the Carolean ceiling was not good. The ceiling was down; a very large number of ceiling joists were fractured. Daylight streamed through a hole in the roof and three or four hip baths full of rainwater explained why the magnificent ceiling below remained intact.

Robert's expansive flow ran unchecked throughout our tour, "My sitting room, the two main spare rooms, two more bathrooms in here, a service lift, staff bathrooms, the kitchen, the red dining room, the green dining room, the saloon, the cold store, a little room where I can cook in front of the camera, somewhere to hang my fabulous Rubens."

My head began to spin, trying to do the mental arithmetic. At a juncture, Norman and Charles appeared carrying by its two handles what appeared to be an ancient laundry basket.

"Here we come!" said Norman cheerfully. "Dot and Doreen, the dinner ladies."

Robert turned to his driver who had been hovering in the background, "Jo, take this down to the harness room. You know where. We'll have lunch at one o'clock maybe. Plenty of wood down there so get the fire lit. OK?" And, turning back to the boys, "Come on! We've had some great ideas and Claire says why don't we make the front room the bathroom (Jack says no problem drainwise) and that pretty little shell cupboard would be in the dressing room. Come and have a look again!"

I excused myself. I really seriously wanted to go and have a look at the roof. I crawled through a forest of rafters and lay on my back looking at the underside of boarded gutters. I walked the length of the parapet; I looked at the fractured beam over the saloon, traced the source of the dry rot smell. There was a hell of a lot of things that needed to be done but the renewal of the roof coverings in whole was not amongst them. The patch over the Carolean room was urgent. I guessed that the oily Mr. Thornton judged the whole of the roof by that small area.

I walked to the back of the house and looked down on the nettle-strewn stable yard. I began to form a number of ideas and began to do a few sums. For a moment I passionately wished Ron was there. I determined at the first possible opportunity to reinforce my views with his. I looked at my watch and saw, guiltily, that it was already a quarter past one and hurried my way down through the empty rooms, through the creeper-covered back door and hoped that I was heading in the general direction of the harness room. I was.

Guided by a roar of conversation, the boom of Robert's laugh pierced by Claire's voice, the fluting tones of Charles and Norman, I opened the door on a cosy scene.

The harness room was delightful. Panelled in vertical boarding, it was surrounded by saddle trees and the faded painted names of long deceased horses. A table had been laid with a snow white double damask table cloth and on this an elegant lunch: Bloor Derby plates, heavy Victorian silver handled cutlery, a noble game pie, a Stilton cheese, a pat of butter with a cow impressed in the middle of it, a glass bowl containing pears in wine. Two bottles of chablis misted with cold stood on the table while an uncorked burgundy had been set to come to room temperature on the floor.

"Hi, there! Come on in," said Robert. "Here's our fabulous architect. Sit down and tell us what you know or shall we have lunch first?"

We had lunch first. As soon as this had been neatly cleared by Charles and Norman into their laundry basket and cups and saucers had been laid with a fat white coffee pot and a humble milk bottle, Claire, who had found a kettle hanging on a hook in the corner, black with age but elegant in the extreme in its eighteenth century contour, elbowed the pugs away from their seat in front of the fire and proceeded to make coffee for the party.

As soon as the tempo changed in this way, Robert, Charles and Norman changed with it. In my ignorance, I had, up till then been deceived by the impression which Robert had so carefully given, into supposing that he had bought the house, almost unseen and on an impulse, that he had hardly looked into the structural complications and had spent the morning pulling ideas out of the air. Such was very far from the case. Both he and the boys had studied the matter with ruthless and cold-hearted detail and knew exactly where they were going. A vital instrument in the ensuing discussion was a particularly good survey and report on the general condition of the structure supplied by an internationally known firm of surveyors in London. I could hardly fault it save in respect of the roof covering and I totally supported (and was infinitely relieved to have) their schedule of approximate costings, leading to a total over all of a little under a hundred and fifty thousand pounds. The thirty thousand pounds my modified proposals in respect of roof coverings would save knocked away a small stone which, in its turn, led to the displacement of a large stone, followed by another, followed by an avalanche, an avalanche under which, driven by Robert's abounding energy, I was almost to be engulfed over the ensuing months.

VIII

Cameron's Kitchen (Part 2)

"Just why the Hell," I said to Byam, "you should suppose that you would be better at this job than I, I simply can't imagine!"

This, as may be guessed, followed half an hour or so of expostulation and complaint from Byam that I should have dropped in for this prestigious job while he was left handling a contract of infinitely less glamour.

"Serve you right!" I said. "Teach you to keep your sticky little fingers to yourself in future!"

Ron and Heather were extremely entertained by this turn of events which left Byam, for once in his life, speechless to protest. The only solid point he was able to make, having been finally driven into the corner by the derision of the office staff was, "You don't know what you're taking on! I've had a damned sight more experience of the rich and spoilt than you have! You just think you're writing an additional chapter for 'Mansfield Park' but this is going to be more like an additional chapter to 'The Castle of Otranto'. Or vol. two of 'Les Liaisons Dangereuses'!"

It was apparent to me that, in the face of Robert's determination to open in June, we were going to be terribly short of time. After intense conference with Ron, I advised, and Robert accepted, that the normal processes of building contract just could not be gone through in the time available and it was agreed that we should negotiate with the most prominent and well established of the Ipswich contractors towards a cost plus fixed fee contract on a draft bill of quantities. This was just Ron's sort of thing. The middle management in this outfit were very much his cup of tea. Vastly experienced, old-fashioned (conceited be it added) figures with whom he was able to negotiate and converse in a condescending and elliptically knowing way, very agreeable to both sides.

We divided the work in this way - Ron and Kirsten settled happily down to the less spectacular contract arrangement, I did most of the more detailed drawings and practically all the P.R. It might have been expected that Robert would be a time-consuming client but such was very far from the case. Very busy himself, he expected no-one to waste his time and he certainly never wasted any of ours. The Local Planning Authority could hardly have been more co-operative. Only too delighted to find a worthy use for the most outstanding house in their district, bureaucratic delays hardly occurred. There seemed likely to be one delay and that concerned the matter of English Heritage grant. As a grade one listed building of the very first order it seemed probable that we should be able to negotiate a state grant towards the repairs of somewhere between forty and sixty per cent of the cost. I had told Robert as much, but this was still in some measure dependent on the favour of an official called Bertram Wickens.

"Wickens here. Bertram Wickens," was his invariable introduction to himself. (It was impossible to imagine anyone addressing him as Bertie.) His colleagues at the Department agreed that he had never been known to smile. I wondered uneasily what would be the confrontation between the ebullient Robert and the puritanical Bertram and looked forward uneasily to his first visit of inspection.

"Bring him to lunch," said Robert. "That's the way to deal with these guys. Fill him up with a good lunch and he'll eat out of your hand!"

I wasn't sure. "Don't overdo it, Robert," I begged. "Some sandwiches, a jug of orange juice, a cup of decaff. - no more than that."

"Ah, Jesus! A glass of water and a dog biscuit," muttered Robert.

I wasn't at all sure he'd got the message.

I met Bertram Wickens at Ipswich station ("10.52. Don't be late," he had said, in memory of an occasion when Byam in similar circumstances had been about three minutes late.) and said, "Mr. Cameron has asked us to lunch."

"I shan't have time for lunch," said Bertram Wickens predictably. "I have to catch the three o'clock or the four o'clock at the very, very latest."

"Well it won't be much," I said pacifically. "Got to stop sometime!"

After a very long morning indeed, partly inspecting the building and partly sitting in conference with the quantity surveyor, we reached a fair measure of agreement on admissible works and modes of repair, and I began to think I had made good progress, though I was uneasily aware of the lunch hanging over us. At one o'clock we repaired to the little Justice Room and my worst forebodings were realised. Although the day was cold, the sun was shining, the window was slightly open, silken curtains stirred in the breeze. A blazing fire offset the winter chill and three Hepplewhite chairs sat hospitably round a Pembroke table in the surface of which a large bunch of winter-sweet was reflected. There were five knives and forks on either side of the gold-rimmed plates and at each table setting were three glasses. Deferentially smiling, two waiters stood with their backs to the wall.

"Really! I don't have time for all this!" said Bertie with even less than his normal charm.

"Ah, come on," said Robert, coming forward with outstretched hand, expansive and hospitable. "A guy's got to eat! It's only a little snack anyway. Let's all have a glass

86

of champagne shall we? Just the thing on a day like this. And then I thought we'd have a bottle of Hermitage with the pheasant. I remember the first time I ever drank it in Burgundy when I was a student..."

A long and involved story followed, punctuated by gales of laughter from Robert, during the course of which Bertram took an austere sip, shook out a crackling napkin the size of a bedsheet and gingerly took his place on the edge of his chair.

Robert introduced the meal with more laughter, several pointed stories, one or two of them quite surprisingly rude. Bertram, to my astonishment, contributed a nutty little jest of his own and the only reference made to the purpose of the visit was when Robert mentioned the need to get on with the roof repairs if damage was not to occur to the Carolean ceiling. Bertram surprised me by uttering a shrill giggle and said,

"'Taedet caeli convexa tueri,' Ha, ha, ha!"

Robert joined in with a burst of laughter. I was perfectly certain that he hadn't the faintest idea what was meant, any more than I had myself. I saved him from any possible following embarrassment by asking for a translation.

"It becomes dispiriting, constantly to watch the arch of Heaven," said Bertram, spluttering with giggles. "Virgil. Aeneid. Book 4, I believe."

At last and some two hours later, "That's all there is," said Robert. "I don't think one should eat too much in the middle of the day, do you? Just a little petit pot de chocolat to finish and I thought we'd have perhaps a glass of Tokay."

Harebell shaped glasses on needle-slim stems appeared on the table and a curiously misshapen bottle of seemingly fabulous antiquity more than liberally decorated with double-headed Imperial eagles began to circulate.

"Mr. Cameron," said Bertram owlishly, "the last applicant with whom I had luncheon thought it necessary to demonstrate his poverty by putting out a slice of beetroot, a slice of Spam, a cold potato and a glass of water for me. May I tell you how infinitely I prefer your technique?"

Without the slightest flicker of triumph Robert's eyes slid across mine and without further comment Bertram Wickens slid beneath the table.

"Nice guy," said Robert. "Why'd anybody say he was difficult?"

I don't suppose the Timperlys lunch truly or extensively influenced the outcome of our grant negotiation, for Mr. Wickens was indeed austere of heart but the grant when it arrived was a very satisfactory one.

Robert's requests and changes of intention now flowed but they were always practical and Ron hauled them on board, coiled them down and paid them out to the building squad in a series of succinct memoranda and a series of typically rough but neat and economical details. And so we proceeded in this way until a day came when, without preamble, Robert's booming voice came over the telephone, "Good morning! And how's Sir Christopher Wren this morning? Say - I'm giving a little Christmas party; nothing much - about a hundred or so, I guess. On December the 15th. Okay? You'll need to get the john connected up and decorated and we'll need a few coats of emulsion in the hall. And - hey Jack - get that shed by the garages out of the way - there'll be fifty plus cars in the stable yard and, the way things are, they'd get in but they'd never get out. Sure, by the end of the evening they'd knock it down for us but perhaps we'd better clear the way for them. Okay?

I had learned by now that it was no good saying 'I'll do my best,' so I said dutifully, "Okay, Robert," rang off and instantly redialled.

My Ipswich contractors had by now very much got the idea. They made no bones about Robert's proposition but I was myself concerned that a Christmas party for somewhere in the region of a hundred people was about to take place in a house in which no one had slept for about twenty years, in a house without central heating and with only the most unreliable electricity and a very large hole (protected by tilts it is true) in the roof of the west wing.

I needn't have worried. The party was a success. The quick coat of emulsion over the entrance hall had hardly had time to dry but, filled with flowers and blazing with candles, floored with two or three large Persian Garden carpets and quivering with music from the six-piece band in the gallery, it was hard to believe that the rest of the house was piled with scaffold planks, concrete mixers, acroprops, shovels, expanded metal lath, sacks of plaster piles of bricks as the unwary, on wandering away from the party, were to find to their cost.

Robert stood in the hall in a crimson robe of a vaguely ecclesiastical flavour greeting his guests with the words, "Ladies' powder room's at the end of the passage. Mind how you go - there's a loose man-hole cover. But if you want the boys' room, you'll have to wait till next year. You just go through the little door beside the fireplace in the saloon and have a slash in the garden. Anything more serious and I'm afraid you have to go home."

The tour de force was in fact the saloon, hung with tapestry "borrowed" by the boys, the most enormous Christmas tree I've ever seen and, in each of the cavernous marble fireplaces at either end of the room, it seemed the whole of an apple tree was blazing cheerfully.

The food, all brought down from Camerons - Robert's restaurant in Sloane Square was non pareil. By the end of the party there was an avenue of empty champagne bottles on which Robert's obese and asthmatic pugs peed disdainfully throughout the party stretching from the entrance hall down the yellow passage beyond the entrance to the Ladies' Powder Room, so-called.

The company was glittering and, with Robert's easy acquiescence, we brought Kirsten and Byam with us. Robert made my evening on introduction to Byam by saying, "So you work for my fabulous architect, do you? Make yourself at home Brian. Great to see you."

Although this was the grandest, and it certainly succeeded in its primary purpose which was to attract the maximum publicity for Timperlys, it was only the first of many similar occasions. I would go over for a site meeting at least once and sometimes as often as two or three times a week to find that a room had rapidly been decorated and furnished, pictures were hanging on the walls, expensive curtains were held in position with tacks and Robert sat at ease amongst the considerable, though temporary splendour being interviewed by the BBC, by Anglia TV, by Australian Vogue, by Paris Match.

The builders loved this, of course, and jostled to be seen walking casually across the back of the scene. Many took to carrying a comb against such photo opportunities.

Early in the proceedings we completed Robert's first priority requirement of 'a room where I can be filmed cooking'. "That work top of yours? How high is it?" he said to me one day.

"Three foot."

"How high's three foot?"

I showed him.

"That's no goddam good! Get yourself photographed behind a thing like that - you're all balls and fly buttons! Make it three foot three. No - three foot four."

We did.

Winter turned to spring and spring almost turned to summer. At one point there were thirty men working on the house which was shrouded in scaffolding and at times it seemed we would never get done. Ron and the general foreman were, however, quite confident.

"Always provided his nibs doesn't change his mind more than six times between now and next Friday," said Ron. "I guess we might just about make it."

The garden was planned and we called Sir Hastings in to do a bird's eye perspective of the ensemble as it might be when finished. He produced in almost no time at all a magnificent drawing which he decorated with an imperial figure in the foreground, recognisable as Robert, a figure kneeling at his feet and unrolling a drawing recognisable as myself.

"Robert's wonderful!" said Claire one evening.

"Robert's nothing of the sort!" I said testily. "Robert's a bloody nuisance!" It had been one of those days.

"He's not," said Claire. "I think he's nearly the perfect client. Scorpio, you know."

"It's all very well for you," I said, "running up and down to London, matching little bits of fabric, arguing with curtain makers, drinking cups of coffee..."

Indeed, Claire was having the time of her life. She became the link between Robert and his many suppliers. She reminded me of the things that I might have forgotten; she tried a bit of furniture here, carried it upstairs and tried it there in shrill conference with Norman and Charles and under the all-organising, all-seeing eye of Robert.

Perceptibly, the day to which all our efforts had been preliminary drew alarmingly close, the day, that is, when Timperlys restaurant opened to the public. The hype had been incessant. When it came to advance publicity Robert was a master. Hardly a day passed when there was not a flattering reference in the daily press, never a week passed when one of the glossies had not picked up the theme. A fortnight before the opening it was a sell-out, all tables booked.

Robert had decided on fairly slender evidence that his opening day coincided with the two hundred and fiftieth anniversary of a famous occasion when royalty had been entertained in the house and had decided for this occasion the restaurant staff should be in the costume of the mid-eighteenth century and that the string band (similarly kitted out) should discreetly discourse Mozart through the evening. The costumes were charming. Claire tried one on to Robert's admiration. We decided she looked like part of the chorus of 'the Marriage of Figaro'.

"Unisex, you see," said Robert. "The same for the girls as for the boys. That ought to photograph well."

I had booked a table for ourselves sometime before and decided that we would go in strength, Claire and me, Byam and Kirsten. Hastings was away, Ron refused and Heather never went out in the evening.

Deliberately we arrived early. Foolishly perhaps I put a screwdriver in my pocket. Well you never know! I could just imagine for example that the notices might not have been put up on the loo and there might be other things lying around loose.

I still, in my heart, thought of Timperlys as a building site so it was a shock to see it on this evening in full war paint. The flowers, the candles, the table settings, the eighteenth century-liveried flunkies, the orchestra tuning up - all this was magic to me. So accustomed was I to seeing the kitchen empty, cold and deserted it was, absurdly, with much surprise that I found it teeming. There is nothing so impressive as professional chefs cooking. The speed, the banging and slapping, the miraculously rapid chopping and slicing, the confidence with which what would seem to me to be vital matters were left to the last or beyond the last possible minute - it was a hive and we were in the way.

We inspected the dining rooms, brilliant with flowers, scented with fruitwood logs in the fireplaces. Four waiters were moving discreetly here and there applying the final touches.

"Four waiters?" said Kirsten wonderingly. "Is that going to be enough?"

I turned to one of them. "Only four of you?" I asked.

He looked gloomily back at me. "There are six more coming down from London but they ought to be here by now," he said. "It'll be a right bloody shambles if they don't turn up. Tell you what - you may find yourselves with your sleeves rolled up yet!"

We walked on, Kirsten and Byam admiring as they went, Claire and I smug and self-congratulatory. We encountered Robert in the hall. He didn't look dismayed, he didn't look ruffled but he looked as nearly both those things as I had ever seen him.

"Problem?" I asked.

"Where's goddam Gidea Park, I'd like to know?" he said, seemingly irrelevantly.

"A12, South Essex. About fifty miles away I'd guess."

"Well," said Robert heavily, "you may be interested to know that the minibus with six waiters on board has just taken a phone box out by the roots in Gidea Park. Jack, you never heard me say this before but I'll say it now - it's a crisis!"

"Bad crisis?"

"The worst, I guess. We've got the key players here but we've only got four waiters. They're good but they can't wait on a goddam hundred!"

We were standing in the cloakroom between the kitchen and the staff restroom. In ranks the waiters' livery hung neatly on the wall beside us.

"Where do I find six waiters half an hour before dinner in the middle of Suffolk on a Saturday night? Can anybody tell me that?"

We looked at each other in consternation. At least three of us looked at each other in consternation. Kirsten did not.

"I do not know where you'll find six waiters Mr. Cameron," she said in her prim little voice, "but I do know where you'll find four."

She ran her hand along the coat hooks beside us, selected the smallest livery coat she could find and slipped her arms into it.

"Of course!" said Claire searching the pegs.

"Steady on," I said. "Kirsten! Claire! Do you know anything about waiting?"

"I do," said Kirsten confidently. "I spent one summer waiting in the canteen at the Harvard Summer School."

"And I," said Byam, peeling off his dinner jacket, "spent one vacation waiting in a trattoria in Portofino."

"I," said Claire, "have never waited in my life but I've always wanted to try! Come on, Jack, what about you?"

"Oh, me," I said nervously, "I'm rather more the arty type you know."

Robert had remained silent throughout this exchange, looking from one to the other and in particular at Claire and Kirsten ferreting about amongst the coats and breeches. Some would have said, 'No, no, you mustn't' or, 'You really don't have to bother,' or something fatuous of that nature but this was not Robert's way. It was a crisis. We were all involved. He would have done the same for us. He let it roll, opening the kitchen door to call, "Jules! Hey, come here a moment!"

A tall, pale, bony individual, half in and half out of a livery coat came swaying towards us. "Jules Lestoq," said Robert. "My Maître d'Hôtel. Jules, these are your stand-by waiters. Only four of them I'm afraid, two with experience. Tell them what to do. The rest of the guys won't be here for an hour at the earliest. Can do?"

"Aw Gawd!" said Jules.

I had expected a throaty Montmartre accent.

"Aw Gawd!" he repeated. "It only ****ing needed that did'n' it? But there we go. Beggars can't be bleedin' choosers. Get changed and I'll tell you what to do."

And so, in an atmosphere of surprising intimacy, we began to disrobe. Neat little cocktail dresses were hung on hangers as were dinner jackets and their attendant trousers. Bow ties gave place to jabots; breeches were struggled into as were white stockings. I took a tricorne hat from a peg, tried it on, imagined it falling into the soup and decided to do without it.

Robert who had watched this transformation burst into a roar of laughter, "Well, goddamit!" he said. "You look great, you guys! There's always a way! Look, I must go - I must be front of house."

"Good luck, Robert," said Claire and, standing on tip toe, she gave him a kiss.

We admired ourselves in the glass.

"I think I look like Dandini," said Claire with satisfaction.

"Dandildo, more like," murmured Jules.

"Something wrong here," said Byam, and, turning to Jules, "You don't have such a thing as a razor, do you?"

"Oh, Byam, no!" said Claire.

"This is a time for sacrifice," said Byam. "And, anyway, whoever saw a Mozart chorus boy in a handlebar moustache? Lead me to it."

As a matter of fact, I thought Claire and Kirsten looked wonderful, especially Kirsten who, Claire and I agreed, looked exactly like Cherubino. Byam looked good too, wincing with pain from his recent déboisement but filled with icy calm. Jules, who along with his uniform coat had assumed for the evening the Montmartre accent I had been expecting, led us through our paces, introduced us to the other waiters, assigned each of us to a waiting team and rapidly explained the well-oiled Cameron system. He told us what not to do and what not to say and stationed us round the dining room.

Robert flashed in for a moment to inspect. "Great!" he said. "Just great! And remember - smile! I say it all the time to these guys don't I?" He turned to the other waiters. "Just smile all the time. If anybody says anything to you - smile. If anybody doesn't say anything to you - smile. And here we go! Stand by to repel boarders!"

"Fix bayonets," said Byam.

"Et gare á tes fesses mon ami," muttered Jules darkly.

The glitterati swarmed on board and the show began.

There were tables composed of County couples, red faces and cheerful, confident voices, many of them ready to remember the last occasion they had dined in this room.

"Twenty years ago," I heard them say. "It must have been

twenty years ago! The last time we were here it was for Lettice Laird-Bennet's wedding, wasn't it?"

"No, no. Hunt ball in 76."

"No, John, surely not."

There were many tables of bright, chattering London couples; there were some French people; there were some Dutch. There was an all male table presided over by Norman and Charles. I thought Norman would have a heart attack when he caught sight of Claire in her outfit. "Oh, darling!" he said, indicating me with a thumb, "if he's mean to you, you know where you can come! Always a welcome from Aunty Norman. Love the breeches!"

The press was there in force and so was smart London. An alarmingly posh gourmet journalist even arrived by helicopter. Some guests were attractive, some hideous, all were expensively dressed. Some came determined to enjoy themselves, some came to louse it up if they possibly could. Robert looked in from time to time and proceeded on these occasions to perambulate the room.

I heard a brassy lady say in a penetrating voice, "I did enjoy your book, Mr. Cameron, but I must say I still prefer Elizabeth David."

"Of course," said Robert, undismayed, "many of the older generation do." He moved on down the tables.

"Don't run," I heard him say out of the corner of his mouth to Kirsten. "Glide!"

Kirsten and Claire were very good at waiting, it seemed to me. Byam, really, I believe, might have been doing it all his life.

"Number 15?" I heard him say in acknowledging a wine order. "The Dopff et Irion riesling? Perfect with the trout. An excellent choice, Sir. I see you know your Alsace wines."

I was very bad at waiting. I got hot, I got bothered, I couldn't remember orders, I apologised in strangled tones to a black velvet evening bag as I squashed it under my slippered foot. I could never remember which side to approach from. I was finally, and to my relief, replaced by Jules.

"This isn't quite your thing, is it dear?" he said. "Tell you what, go and stand in the hall. Here's your list. Take it and tick their names off when they come through the door. Point them the right way to their table. That's all you have to do." Much to my relief - and to the relief of my customers too no doubt - he took over my slot in the dining room and I stationed myself by the front door looking as much like a devoted retainer as I could manage.

"Tick their names off and point them to their table," Jules had said. That's all I had to do. I read my way down the list and towards the end I came to, laconically, 'H.R.H. Party of six. Table 21.' Or was it table 27? And was this H.R.H. male or female? Would I recognise him or her? Suddenly my job did not seem to be a sinecure. Presumably if it was a male H.R.H. I said 'Sir' but if it was a female H.R.H.? I dared not leave my post to consult Jules.

I needn't have worried. The arrival of the royal party was signalled by a blaze of headlights through the front door and a crunch of gravel signifying three or possibly four cars. At that precise moment and with the air of one who just happened to be walking through the hall by chance at that very moment, Robert appeared.

With a series of courtly bows and a flurry of handshakes he gathered up the royal party and shepherded them unhesitatingly to table 21. I was left holding a very large number of coats, wondering what I was supposed to do with them.

Next to arrive was a hired minibus load of waiters who zipped in through a side entrance and announced themselves to me. Scruffy in jeans and trainers, they looked disdainfully about them. I conducted them, shrugging and grumbling, through to the changing room and indicated the ranks of livery. "You're supposed," I said, "to put this lot on." And I hurried away. About ten minutes later they reappeared, transformed, and took their place efficient and smiling under the wing of Jules in the dining rooms.

Kirsten and Claire emerged, flushed and bright-eyed, to be followed after a short interval by Byam. I saw him pause as he passed through the dining room to gather up a bucket with a bottle of champagne in it.

"Where are you going with that?" I asked him.

"Not where am I going - where are we going," he said. "There's a little sort of squalor beyond the kitchen dignified by the title of staff rest-room. If we elbow some of the brimming ash trays aside we could perhaps have a little sit, to say nothing of this excellent bottle of champagne. (I wonder who it was meant for?) I don't know about you but I need a break. My feet are killing me!"

"Real waiters are wonderful," said Claire. "I don't know how they do it!"

"I thought you lot were pretty wonderful," I said. "I couldn't do it at all!"

We settled down round the table to compare our experiences. I told them how elegantly I had received royalty, Claire said someone had asked her for her phone number, a restaurateur from Great Yarmouth had offered Byam a job and Kirsten had been groped by one of Norman and Charles' guests. "But he was looking for something he was never going to find," she said in her neutral little voice.

The door of our snuggery opened to reveal Robert, champagne bottle in hand. "There you are!" he said. "Been looking for you guys everywhere. Time for another drop of the Widow, I think - I see you've already made her acquaintance. How do you think it's going?"

We reassured him, "Wonderful!" we said. "Absolutely wonderful!"

"Mmm.. the hot oysters with coriander weren't much, but the feuilletée of chanterelles was the best I've ever tasted I think," he said with satisfaction. "Everybody loved it." He poured himself out a glass of champagne. "You guys are off watch now," he said. "Want some dinner?"

Dinner suddenly seemed like a very good idea indeed.

"Do you think there'll be any chocolate sushi left?" asked Claire anxiously.

I burned the champagne cork in a candle.

"Before we go back on stage again - the moustache?" I said to Byam. "Want me to sketch it in for you?"

We changed back into our evening dress and I thought we all looked pretty ordinary again. We were, however, conducted by Robert in person to our table and since the royal party had been the only other one to receive this attention, our entrance did not go unremarked.

"They think we're royalty," said Claire excitedly.

"Funny old royalty!" I said.

"Not funny at all," said Byam, inclining his head graciously to left and right. "Soigné, distingué and élégant. They assume that I am a Spanish prince."

"They assume I'm the bodyguard," I said morosely.

"And they think I'm the au pair girl on her evening out," said Kirsten.

"Nonsense," said Byam. "They take you for my little daughter. The fruit of an indiscreet mésalliance, of course."

"Well, Papa, perhaps I should tell you that your moustache is running down your royal chin," said Kirsten crisply.

We were handed enormous menus - each, I guessed, about A3 size. They were decorated with a flower-swagged baroque cartouche from which amorini tumbled down the margins. Only one of these had prices on it and the priced copy was handed to me.

"They don't think you're royal," I said to Byam. "They think I am. Look, I've got the priced menu."

"No, no," said Byam. "As the bodyguard you will be responsible for paying. Like me, royalty never carry money."

The dinner was excellent. Bar none the best dinner I have ever had. Course followed course and each lasted a very long time. Little subsidiary courses appeared unbidden between the main courses, empty wine bottles were whisked away and replaced with others. I was astonished as this fabulous meal drew to a conclusion to notice through the window that it was nearly daylight. Kicking off her shoes and leaning back with uncharacteristic abandon, Kirsten surveyed the room. Crimson faces, bibulous laughter, unfocussed eyes, slightly disarranged finery were noted with a touch of Calvinistic disapproval. Robert came to join us for a moment.

"All that effort..." Claire said.

"And what an effort!" Robert said.

Kirsten picked up the theme. "All that effort - the painting, the glazing..." Briefly her eye took in the freshly marbled ceiling, the floorboarding painted and glazed to simulate paving, the newly carved baroque mirror, the trompe l'oeil panels. "All those weeks of work, all those drawings, all that skill," she said disparagingly, "a means - and to what an end! All these people troughing away! Do you know - at one of my tables they had a £500 drink bill! £500! Can you imagine? All that effort was the means and this is the end!" She waved a slightly unsteady hand around the room.

"No," said Robert seriously. "You've got it the wrong way up. All these guys and - okay, I agree by the sober light of dawn they don't look much - all these guys are the means but the food, the drink, the setting - that's what it was all about. Builders, decorators, plasterers, upholsterers, chefs, waiters - all given a chance to do their thing! Creative, that's what we were. These guys, they'll get their chequebook out at the end of the day and provide the means. They've had a good time and we've had a good time creating the good time! And the house! Back to life again, wouldn't you say? Oh, no - the house was the end."

IX

Jolly Boating Weather.

Sir Hastings' sunny self-confidence and complacent rotundity made it hard sometimes to believe that he had ever been other than as we see him today. It was impossible to imagine him at a loss or at a disadvantage; impossible to imagine his professional judgement in doubt. For these reasons it was always refreshing when his vein of discursive reminiscence revealed a shore on which he had nearly run aground, a rock he had been lucky to circumnavigate or that there could ever have been anyone prepared to give him the run-around in a way so familiar to Byam and me.

It was good, therefore, when, during a visit together to a university city of legendary architectural distinction, he stopped dead in his tracks and rocked back on his heels looking upwards at the towering bulk of the mediaeval wall encircling the ancient church of St. Martin.

"There!" he said, waving his hand with a proprietorial air. "What do you think of that, my boy?"

A difficult question to answer in a word.

What could I say? - 'It's large. It's tall. It's old. It's covered with creeper and stone crop. It's leaning dangerously out over the street and -' as I looked upwards, I could have added, 'it seems to be supporting a large number of mature trees.'

"What do I think? Well, I think it looks pretty unstable. Is that what we've come to look at?"

"Unstable? Nothing of the sort! Stuff and nonsense! Sound as the day it was built. Probably sounder if anything."

It was hard to believe him. The wall in question overhung the pavement by a foot or more and though not a busy road, the citizenry passed to and fro in large numbers - as I should judge - in peril of their lives.

"Are you sure?" I asked nervously.

"Sure? Absolutely sure! Tell you a story..." said Sir Hastings cosily. "Roman construction in the base courses at least. Look - there... and there. Roman bricks, my boy. Roman masonry. And that," he pointed, "Know what it is? I'll tell you. Roman tombstone. Built into the wall."

"Yes, I appreciate all that but I ask again - is it safe?"

Sir Hastings resumed, "Forty years ago the church rang me up in a terrible flap. They'd been told the wall wasn't safe, that it was their responsibility, there was a danger to life and limb, they'd been told it would have to be rebuilt, the trees would have to come down and they'd been told it would cost somewhere in the region of a hundred thousand pounds. A lot of money in those days. Quite a lot of money today come to think of it... So I came and had a look. Took a few measurements; dropped a tape over the top; walked around the churchyard; scratched me head; went away to write a report. Gloomy sort of document. Wrapped it up as best I could but the plain conclusion was that the poor St. Martin's Church were going to have to rebuild their wall - lose a lot of churchyard - lose their lime trees - close the road for about three months while the work was in hand. Didn't add up to very good news, however you looked at it. Didn't realise it at the time but I was about to put me head in a wasps' nest!

"Anyway, I came into the office a couple of days later and found Ron reading my report. Well, you know Ron! 'Looks like we've got a nice little earner 'ere,' says he. 'Nice little earner, nothing!' I said. 'These blokes haven't got any money at all! Nice little loser more like.'

"In those days Ron read everything that came into the office. All the bumphlets you know. Don't suppose he bothers nowadays; got like me - thinks he knows it all. Well, 'Come and have a look at this,' he says and he produces a catalogue from some Italian outfit. Well I don't speak much Italian and Ron doesn't speak any at all but the substance of it was that there was on the market a system stabilising dangerous mediaeval fabric. When it comes to the point, of course, the Italians probably know all there is to know about dangerous mediaeval fabric! And, when you come to think of it, there are probably more Roman walls on the point of collapse in Italy than anywhere else in the world so I had a more careful look.

"'Might work,' says Ron. 'Cheaper than knocking it down and starting again,' and I began to think he had a point.

"It was an ingenious system. What you did was this - you drilled a series of diagonal holes downwards through the face of the wall with a high pressure hose. When you reckoned you'd got down far enough, you jacked up the water pressure so there was a sort of cavity at the end of your diagonal hole."

Oblivious to the occasionally passing traffic, Sir Hastings extracted a pad from his pocket and began to draw. "Like this, you see. And you feed some high tensile steel wires down into the shaft, fill it up with concrete and there you are - internal guy ropes, holding the wall together. Not cheap but perhaps one tenth of the cost of rebuilding the wall."

Without moving from the middle of the road, Sir Hastings continued to explain, genially waving the traffic past as each car made a detour round him.

"Anyway, the job started. We started to drill these holes. As far as I can remember there were about thirty of them, all over the face of the wall. Never had such a messy job in all my life. Water pouring down, mud all over the road, complaints from everybody in sight but mostly from the City Engineer. Aggressive sort of chap. Perhaps I hadn't exactly explained what we were up to. Perhaps I was a bit off-hand. Not very tactful in those days but I don't suppose you can imagine that."

I could.

"He decided he'd sort me out - bumptious young London architect. It began to look as if he'd close the job and finally he closed the road. Just as well. Noise was pretty deafening too. Began to wonder if I'd done the right thing but the engineer chappie in charge of the job from the contractor's end was pretty relaxed. 'Always happens,' he said. 'You can't do this sort of thing without making a bit of a mess.' I thought, 'All very well for you but you haven't got to explain this to the neighbours or the press.' The rector didn't like it much either. It was making him very unpopular. Oh well, you get a job like this sometimes. You just have to keep your head down." A ruminant smile. "Keep your head down. We do it all the time!

"I went down there one day and there they were, belting this concrete with some magic in it to retard the set down into the latest shaft. Chemistry you know - didn't understand as much as half of all that. 'How much have you put in there?' I asked, not really wanting to know but one tries to take an intelligent interest. 'Fifty bags,' he says. '- That's a lot. None of the others have taken more than five.'

"Well I didn't know much about it but I took it on myself to say, 'Stop. Leave that one out of it. There's a void in there somewhere and you're filling it up with concrete. May be an old cellar, a crypt or something, a Roman drain even. Forget it.' The engineers didn't like it very much but when all was said and done, I was the boss and I couldn't see that it would matter too much if we missed one of these things out. Seemed to me they'd been scattering them about like grass seed... probably an overkill anyway. Well, while I was standing there wondering if I'd done the right thing, the City Engineer comes along, accompanied by his minions.

"'How much longer are you going to be?.. Can't put up with this mess much longer... Complaints about the noise... Question of damages...' You can imagine the sort of thing. Forty years ago I was a bit younger than I am now. When you get to my age you can get away with murder but maybe I didn't look very impressive. Maybe I didn't feel very impressive. I think he discovered my weaknesses. He really threw the book at us - no work on site before 9.30 in the morning or after 4 p.m., absolutely no weekend working, rubbish to be cleared up as it accumulated, stop/go traffic signs at either end of the lane, weekly site meetings, had I given notice under this regulation, that regulation or the other? (of course I hadn't)... He really settled in to give me a bad time. Somewhere at the back of my mind came the thought - Fate'll catch up with him!

"But I began to wonder whether these Italian blokes knew what they were up to. Still, I soothed him down as best I could.

"Now, as luck would have it, the next day was a Saturday and this City Engineer was going down the river in a punt with his girlfriend. With his girlfriend, you understand, and that is to some extent the point of the story because he wasn't going down the river with Mrs. City Engineer. Still, even City Engineers have to kick up their heels from time to time, I suppose. Anyway, he came to a shady corner, moored his punt and no doubt unpacked his picnic, uncorked a bottle of wine and so on. He had omitted to notice that just above him and almost invisible because considerably overgrown was a culvert designed to discharge excess storm water into the river.

"And what should happen? Well you've probably guessed. Just tidying up their picnic when there was a slurp and a gurgle and a ton of 1:2:4 concrete came belting out through this culvert and into his punt. Now Thames punts are robust vehicles but they're not really designed to take even half a ton of concrete on board and it wasn't long before the water was rising round their ankles. It wasn't long before their picnic was floating down the river and it wasn't very long before their boat began to sink and in no time at all this unfortunate man and his even more unfortunate girlfriend were swimming for it. Quite a scene as I think you'll agree!

"Well, you don't see the City Engineer swimming fully clothed in the river very often. Made quite a news item!"

"News item? But how did the papers get hold of it?"

His mischievous blue eyes glazed over momentarily with a mist of recollection. "Oh, there's always some fool with a camera hanging over every bridge in the summer... I was there meself that day... Come to think of it, it probably made quite an item for discussion over the family breakfast table but when the excitement had died away the City Engineer began to think. 'Concrete,' he thought, 'now what do I know about concrete? Where did it come from? Don't often find concrete flowing down the city storm water sewers..?' And then, of course, the penny dropped! I can imagine his mind working. 'That scoundrel Munro! Nowhere else it could have come from!'

"I had a telephone call I'd very much rather not have had. What had happened of course was this - the fifty bags that we had put down shaft number 6B had gone into an old drain. A Roman drain probably. No one knew it was there. And being pretty sloppy liquid, slithery stuff it had flowed cheerfully on out of the churchyard, under the street but more cogently into the storm water sewer. And by the time they had established what had happened, the concrete had - because even magic concrete does eventually - set hard. Can you imagine it? The whole dashed storm water system of the city packed out with the best concrete! Good God - they had to dig up the whole road... they had to dig out about fifty yards of sewer... they had to break it out. It lay in columns! The streets were closed, the traffic was diverted and, of course, the question came to me - who's liable?"

Breathlessly, I enquired, "Who was?"

"Well," said Sir Hastings, "as it turned out, the Engineers were responsible and the Contractor was responsible. He was supposed to report the rate of uptake but hadn't done so. Fifty bags indeed!

"It's a funny thing, I always thought, this City Engineer had given me a really bad time, frightened me out of my skin while the job was going on and I'd had many a fantasy about getting even with him one day - and, as you see, I did! Indirectly, of course, but effectively, I think you'll say."

Sir Hastings smiled with reminiscent pleasure. "You don't get a chance to scupper a chap's boat, to say nothing of his romance, every day of the week! I thought, 'He'll think twice before he tangles with Munro again!'"

X

Remember Uncle Willie.

I came into the office one day to find on Byam's desk a large and glossy brochure depicting, on the cover, a large and glossy house. I covered up the caption and tried to see if I could deduce the whereabouts. I guessed that it dated from the 1870's. It was built in the streaky bacon school, that is to say banded red and white brickwork. Clearly not in England. In France? I didn't think so. In Germany perhaps? Again, I didn't think so. Each corner was surmounted by a pepper-pot turret, each turret had a conical roof and on each conical roof the sort of metal flag that is deemed to be a suitable embellishment for a 'maison de maître'. Or would this be a château? Or, depending on its location, a schloss?

The garden was in terrifyingly good order and in the brightly coloured photograph carefully laid out ranks of salvias, petunias, and geraniums seared the eye. Shaven lawns were well supplied; faintly mediaeval statuary lurked in the shade of chiselled yews and an uncomfortable looking fountain spouted in the foreground.

I decided my deductive faculties could do no more and I opened the brochure. I hadn't made a bad shot; it was, in fact, in Belgium and, more particularly in the Ardennes near the French border and the particulars had come from a property agency in Philippeville. I looked at the photograph again and saw that the Château Amberloup was, seemingly, embowered in a dense forest. It was evidently a hotel and it had one Michelin rosette. It had thirty two bedrooms, six reception rooms, central heating, garaging for six and two cottages. Not quite sure what the exchange rate was between the pound and the Belgian franc, I decided in the end that it could be mine for a million pounds. I couldn't imagine why it was lying on Byam's desk.

He came to peer over my shoulder.

"Thinking of going into the hotel business?" I asked. "Yours for about a million."

"No," said Byam meditatively, "at least not on my own account. Interesting though. I can't think why they've sent this thing to me, though, in a manner of speaking, you might say this is my ancestral home, that is to say it did belong to my Great Uncle Willie and before him to his Uncle Hendrick and it was sold just after the war."

"Princely property," I said.

"Oh, yes, but it wasn't always so. I'll tell you....

"My great uncle Willie was a loser. Everything he did turned to mud."

"Turned to mud? With a pad like this?"

"Well it wasn't always like that. Uncle Willie - my grandmother's brother - never had much luck. He was always a family responsibility. His parents were always bailing him out but in spite of this, in 1939, it could be said that ruin stared him in the face."

"What happened?"

"At this low ebb in his fortunes he gets a letter from a lawyer in Philippeville to say that his Uncle Hendrick had died and he, Uncle Willie, had inherited the Château Amberloup. Well, of course, Uncle Willie thinks to himself, 'What ho! This is the stuff!' He knew the house quite well from his childhood holidays spent there though he hadn't visited it for about twenty years. Well the first thing to do was to borrow the fare from somebody and go and inspect his inheritance and this - painfully, I expect - by train and bus he set off to do, having arranged to meet the notaire at the château.

"Well, the first thing was that he'd forgotten how long the drive was and although the bus put him down at the gate he was still confronted by a longish walk through the dripping woods carrying his suitcase I dare say, for about three miles. At last, rounding the corner, he came on the holiday home of his childhood, the focus of so much great expectation. Figure his dismay! Gone the smooth lawns of childhood memory, gone the loyally bobbing domestics at the door, almost gone the château! Sagging roofs, broken glass, displaced guttering, mildew patches all over the brickwork and, perhaps worst of all - which he had not appreciated - no electricity, no mains water and three miles of drive, potholed and, in places, almost impassable to wheeled vehicles. Trees had fallen and lay where they fell. A water rat swam in the cracked fountain basin and, to cap all, a wild boar was perceived to be rooting in what his childhood's memory told him had been the rose garden.

"The notaire stood, impatient, on the doorstep. Uncle Willie was predictably and characteristically three quarters of an hour late for his appointment and, with sinking heart, my poor uncle allowed himself to be shown round. If the exterior was depressing, the interior was disastrous and rendered the more so by the remains of velvet curtains hanging here and there and, ultimately, a tiny little ground floor bedroom (formerly, I'd guess, the butler's pantry or something of that sort) with Uncle Hendrick's pyjamas laid out on a chair and a cup, saucer, plate, knife, fork, spoon and a jar of something that appeared to be yoghourt but had probably once been milk on a small table. He encountered a dry-rot fungus the size of a football.

"One may imagine the shruggings that went on on the part of the notaire. Poor old Uncle Willie sought his advice as to what on earth to do next. You must remember that this was July 1939. · War clouds gathered. Gotterdammerung, you might say. And not only war clouds but storm clouds too because soon their perambulation was to the tune of water dripping here and pouring there through the many holes in the many gutters of the ornamental spiky roofs. Poor Willie! His only comfort in these terrible circumstances was that he could beg a lift to the bus stop from the notaire on the first leg of a depressed return to England.

"However at this dark hour there was comfort. Here was the war and Uncle Willie who'd been out of work off and on for about ten years and being bilingual was suddenly in demand. He dropped into a little slot with the BBC. The château, we must suppose, slipped out of his mind. He had instructed the notaire to put the property on the market or alternatively to let it, instructions received with pitying scorn. (Nothing like a Belgian notaire for evincing pitying scorn.) And so the matter rested until 1945.

"With the end of the war, all the lads coming marching home again, Uncle Willie's temporary job at the BBC folded and it seemed that he was back to where he was in 1939, unemployment, penury and advancing old age. Lonely old age too because Aunt Gretel had recently left him and run off with a flautist in the London Philharmonic - a bad career move as you will shortly hear. Figure his surprise once more, therefore, to have a letter from the notaire. Mystifying document indeed! It said, in effect,

"'Pursuant to your instructions of the 14th of July 1939, we duly let the Château Amberloup and have now £6,000 (or the equivalent in Belgian francs) credited to an account we opened for you at the Banque Populaire in Philippeville. May we have your instructions? Etc. Etc.'

"Uncle Willie's first thought was that the letter had been misaddressed but, shaking with excitement, he dared to make a telephone call. A thing people didn't often do in those days! Ringing up Belgium was a pretty hi-tech activity in 1945. Marvels were not to cease! It appeared that during the German occupation the Wehrmacht had chanced upon the property, had decided that it was just what they wanted to establish a school of forest warfare - perhaps with Barbarossa pending they thought they ought to train up a corps d'élite to battle their way through the trackless forests of Mother Russia. Anyway, be that as it may, they took the property on. They not only took the property on, they brought in water and electricity. They repaired the drive. Above all, they pretty well rebuilt the roof and for all I know they set the fountain working again. They put in things like bathrooms and this, amazing as it might seem, was not all. Conscientiously (and I do think the Germans are extremely odd) they hadn't bothered to enquire who owned the property. It never crossed their minds that the owner might be a pig-like Englishman (Uncle Willie, after all, had a reasonably convincing German surname) and they had virtuously paid the rent into his account in Philippeville!"

Byam reflected for a moment. "The older I get, the more convinced I become that happy endings are few. But when I'm a prey to Weltschmerz I can drum up a spot of Schwärmerei when I consider the luck of it. And when I think of Aunt Gretel walking out on him in the pit of his misfortune I give way to a measure of Schadenfreude. So whatever fate may have in store for us, let us rally to the cry, 'Remember Uncle Willie!'"

"I will!" I said, "I will!"

XI

A Little Accommodation.

In moments of exasperation it often seemed to me that Byam really had a taste for living dangerously. I was often horrified at the corners he was prepared to cut and the risks he was prepared to take. Alternately horrified as I contemplated the possible consequences of this system and alternately gratified (and irritated) as, one by one, his finesses came off. As Ron said on one occasion, "The Devil's children have the Devil's luck."

And so, in the matter of Fitzclarence Street, Mayfair, but only after a nail-biting crisis, this seemed to be proved.

The job in question was an odd one. Byam had an outstandingly creepy client. At least I thought he was creepy but Byam admired him extravagantly. His name was Firbank de Staines and he ran a small wine merchant's business from this prestigious address. I went there once. It seemed entirely staffed by soft-eyed, olive skinned elegant youths in very expensive suits. The customers appeared to be entirely from the Third World.

"Knocking out trade gin to the underprivileged?" I asked. "Is that a respectable activity? Does it not correspond to selling firewater to the Plains Indians?"

"Well, you can put it like that if you want to," said Byam, "but I suppose as any good frontier trader would have claimed - 'If they don't get it from us, they'll get it from someone else.' Anyway, it's no part of my job to check out the morality of my client's business activities."

And it must be admitted that 'Glen Macraevie Auld Scotch Whisky, Triple Distilled in Ghana for the Discerning Palate' sold very well, so well, in fact, that Firbank de Staines decided that it would be a boost to his business and simplify the entertainment of his overseas clients if he had a little guest house in which to put them up when they flew in on buying trips.

At the end of his garden (typical forlorn garden in that part of London - dusty and cat-scrabbled laurels, crumbling bird bath and - on one occasion when I visited - one single daffodil) there stood a two storey structure. Once upon a time I suppose it was coachman's quarters or something of that sort but it consisted of little more than a large room on each of two floors. Byam's instructions were to convert, extend, alter, amend and generally tart up this little building to contain on each floor a lush studio room, a kitchenette, a sumptuous bathroom and a discreet side entrance. The mind did not have to stretch far to accommodate speculation as to the goings-on for which this building as altered was supposed to cater.

Byam had his problems from the outset. De Staines was Janus-headed. Big smile on the one face, spiteful, carping, stingy, changeable and incessantly demanding on the other. He had the devastating habit of working both late and early; he could see no reason why Byam should not attend meetings at two hours' notice or that Byam should not be manning his telephone constantly from eight o'clock to eight o'clock and beyond.

Byam's immediate problem was that there was very little headroom on the ground floor. If you are trying to increase headroom, there are two things you can do - you can, on the one hand, raise the ceiling and you can, on the other hand, lower the floor. All things being equal, the second alternative is likely to be the more economical and this is what Byam set out to do.

"We only need to gain about 300 mil," he said. "Shouldn't be a problem. Floor level's considerably higher than ground level and the floor's got to be renewed anyway."

"Have a little exploratory dig, perhaps?" suggested Ron. "Learned anything from Pitt House, did we? See what it's got in the way of foundations - get the District Surveyor up your knickers and you could have problems. You know what these characters in London can be like. You're not altering a dear little summer house in friendly old Suffolk, you know."

"It'll be okay," said Byam absently.

I worried. Byam's fugitive concentration was at this time even more intermittent than usual as storm clouds gathered over his never very stable love-life, the state of which became, it seemed, increasingly obscure by the day.

And so the job started and such were the restrictions of the site that the dig had to be done by hand and it wasn't five minutes before it was revealed that Byam's little coachhouse had no foundations of any sort at all. It was, in fact, standing on two or three courses of manifestly defective brickwork. Worse than that, it was discovered that it was built over a pit. "Not another one!" groaned Heather. "You and your pits! Still, at least we're insured now!"

Horse-drawn London had a perpetual problem with mounding manure and the solution was to dig a large hole and hope for the best. Byam's coachhouse was standing on just such a pit. The contractors dug and they dug. They went down and they went down. At a depth of about 6'6" (or two metres if you prefer) they extracted and revealed to Byam's somewhat horrified inspection, toothily grinning, the skull of a horse.

"Get rid of the bloody thing," said Byam desperately, with dire visions of having uncovered a site of major archaeological interest.

It became quite clear that the building, if it was to be retained, would need to be underpinned. It was further revealed that conventional foundations would have to descend to a fathomless depth. The alternative was to pile the foundations. The increase in cost was alarming. Vitally important buyers from the Dark Continent were booked in in a very few months' time. Byam received a menacing letter from de Staines' solicitor, touching not lightly on the question of negligence and calculating not sparingly an amount of compensation should the building not be completed by the due date.

However, that surprising man now spun about like a weather-cock, accepted the inevitable extra and let it be understood that, provided the contract was completed in reasonable time, no further action would follow.

Pallid with relief, Byam heaved a deep sigh. So did I. So did Ron.

In circumstances of hideous congestion short bore piles were introduced. The noise was appalling, the vibration considerable. In a mild but peevish sort of way complaints began to come in from adjoining owners. Mild and peevish in respect of the generality of these but very far from mild and much more than peevish in respect of the immediately adjoining owner at the rear of Byam's coachhouse. This was the Fitzclarence Club, a slab-faced, Georgianesque structure circa 1930 on five storeys. Five storeys and a basement.

The basement, unknown to Byam, contained a swimming pool, also, presumably, of the 1930s.

There came a telephone call from a tremendously grand firm of architects - Sir James Ferguson, Sons & Partners, Chartered Architects, writing from four or five floors in Berkeley Square, were at a loss to comprehend how it was that works below ground should be in hand adjoining the Fitzclarence Club whom they represented without the relevant notice having been given under the relevant section of the relevant act.

I explained the possible consequence of this to Claire. "You have a five storey building which is sitting on a basement swimming pool. Your adjoining neighbour proceeds to drive piles down the outside of the separating wall, probably miles below the bottom of the swimming pool. What happens? You wake up one fine morning and find your swimming pool's run off to join the Tye Burn. I can hear it all!"

"Oh, Byam!" said Claire, biting her fist in a way she had when perturbed. "What do they expect him to do about it?"

"Well, quoting the relevant section of the act, threatening Byam with the utmost rigour of the law, at the moment they only ask that there should be a Schedule of Condition drawn up and agreed with respect to the Fitzclarence Club before any further work is done. They blandly observe that it is in Byam's interest to draw up such a document, the idea being that if all or any defects which exist in the Fitzclarence Club are recorded now, then there can be no claim in respect of these, only in respect of any subsequently developed by reason of Byam's nefarious operation."

"You mean that if Byam just goes round there and makes a note of any old cracks they've got already, they will only claim if any new damage occurs? Well, that's all right then. Sounds very reasonable to me."

"It's not as easy as that," I said. "This club has got thirty six bedrooms and they're all let! Byam has to arrange to visit them all. Some he will be able to get access to, others he won't. There's going to be a tremendous amount of 'Come back tomorrow,' or 'Lord Bumpstead won't be back from Africa for another six weeks.' It'll take months to draw up and then it's got to be agreed by this Ferguson outfit! And all the time Firbank de Staines is standing menacingly in the wings with a bottle of Ghana whisky in one hand and a six-shooter in the other!"

Claire contemplated this bizarre information. "I don't

117

think that's difficult," she said finally. "It's impossible."

Impossible it seemed. Of course, I offered to come and help him. Of course, Ron offered. Sir Hastings thought it would probably sort itself out.

"Two days' intensive for all three of us!" I said. "These Fitzclarence boys have got to give us a break! It may not be too bad but you've got to stop work on the coachhouse."

Byam turned green. "I can't," he said. "I can't!"

"You must! You must!"

"I won't! I won't!"

"Fitzclarence will slap an injunction on you if you don't!" said Ron with more austerity than I had ever heard from him and so the matter stood through an alarming weekend.

A weekend during the course of which I had a telephone call from Great Aunt Phyllis. Great Aunt Phyllis rather surprisingly - surprisingly for my family that is - owned a house in Moore Street, Chelsea, now very smart indeed. Forty years ago when she inherited it it had seemed to her that it would be a nice little house in which she could let rooms. Forty years on and rather bemused, she found herself surrounded by merchant bankers, Eurobond operators, Conservative M.P.s, in a word, by the new rich. Such citizens are incapable of moving into a house without laying out about half the purchase price in improvements. There was hardly a house that did not have a builder's board outside it and there was hardly a day when scaffolding did not bristle and compressors did not throb. Aunt Phyllis, however, lived on in the midst of this confusion in a house in which, greatly daring, she had provided no fewer than two bathrooms forty years ago.

"Oh, hello, dear," said a vague but recognisable voice, "Auntie Phyllis here. And how are you?... And little Claire? How's little Claire? Are you busy?"

I told her how I was, how was little Claire and said, yes, I was satisfyingly busy.

"Not too busy, I hope, to come and give me a bit of

advice?"

And this I cordially agreed to do.

"The problem," said Aunt Phyllis, "is with my next door neighbours. They're building a sort of roof garden and conservatory at the back. It takes off quite a bit of my light but I don't want to complain. I wouldn't like any bad feeling before the new people have even moved in. I don't know them. They say he's an M.P. - or would it be a Euro MP? Something like that anyway. They're spending an awful lot of money. But that's not the point. They've been making a terrible noise and of course that's not to be avoided but yesterday a picture fell off the wall in my hall and when I came to look there was the end of a pickaxe sticking through the wall! I went round next door and they were very apologetic. They've filled the hole in and they said it wouldn't happen again but I just wondered whether, well, was that all right? And now some bricks have fallen out at the back. I expect it's all right but I would be so grateful, dear, if you'd come and have a look."

I made a date to visit her on Monday, truth to tell, quite pleased to get out of the office and get away from the unravelling horrors of Fitzclarence Street. A cosy cup of coffee with Aunt Phyllis, a five minute visit to view the works, an affable and condescending discussion with the offending next-door builders and lunch in one of the many little restaurants that abound in that part of London... I would take Claire with me. Worse ways of spending the day, I thought.

I made my way to Moore Street, duly greeted my aunt and left her gossiping with Claire while I went next door. The contractors were contrite in the extreme, didn't know how it could possibly have happened, deeply regretted any inconvenience to my client, would pick up the bill for any making good that might be required... Perhaps they should have notified that they were cutting a considerable pocket from the separating wall to accommodate the beam end of their new balcony...?

We discussed this at length but, aware that they were manifestly in the wrong, they were prepared to fall over backwards to make good. They even offered to renew the stepped flashing in the dividing wall. And - 'While we've got blokes up there,' they said, 'we'll decorate the old lady's roof light for her.'

There seemed to be no shortage of money and I easily persuaded them to repoint the parapet copings while they were at it. Well satisfied with my achievement I collected Claire, told Aunt Phyllis what a clever boy I was, tried without success to return the £50 which she pressed into my hand - ('Don't expect you to work for nothing, Jack') and wandered off to spend it on lunch.

On the way home, while Claire drove, I dictated a minute to the builder and wondered whether I should send a copy to the adjoining owner.

"Do you know his name?" asked Claire and I searched my notes.

"Yes. Sir Hanbury Turner M.P."

"Hanbury Turner!" said Claire. "Oh, he's always in the news. Quite a sleaze bag by all accounts... shady dealings. Isn't he the guy who was concerned with a couple of hundred acres of waste land at Walsall? And the dodgy planning consent for that multi-million pound leisure complex? Isn't he being acutely scrutinised by the Nolan Committee? And while your friend Firbank de Staines may be shipping gin out to Africa, isn't Hanbury Turner busily engaged in selling muskets to people he oughtn't to be selling muskets to in the Gulf? Yes! I'm sure I'm right! That's the chap! Tell you what, Jack, you could sell your story to the 'Mirror' - 'Poor widow lady... wicked plutocrat knocking her foundations from under her without so much as a by-your-leave... massive action for distress caused... I think you've missed a chance! And - this guy Turner - does he have an architect? Go after him! Hassle him a bit! You're too nice, Jack, that's your problem!"

When I got back to the office the following morning, I found Byam alert and wearing his best suit but wan with care.

"Glad you're back!" he said, uncharacteristically. "Got a bit of a party today. Wouldn't do any harm if you were there. The Ferguson mob are coming down in force to discuss our problems at the Fitzclarence. I said I'd go and see them in London but, no, they insisted on coming down to see us. Determined to make our flesh creep, I fear. I don't know what you can say, but if you could just sit there and look severe, competent, knowing a good deal more than you're saying, very ready to quote case law - you know the sort of thing - I'm sure you can do it."

I wasn't by any means sure.

As we sat waiting for our meeting, Heather brought in the memorandum in the matter of Moore Street and Ron, sitting with us for the moment, picked it up and said, "Send a copy to the client, yes, good, but more important, send a copy to the architect. Who is the architect by the way?"

I confessed that I didn't know, picked up the telephone and rang the builder.

Affable to the last, a chatty voice came back.

"Architect? Sir James Ferguson, Sons and Partners. You probably know them? Berkeley Square. We do all their minor works in London. I'm sorry we've had this bit of bother at Moore Street and you can certainly rely on us to put it right. Client is Sir James Ferguson's brother-in-law so it's rather special. So grateful for all your help and co-operation yesterday. You must let us know, of course, if there's anything more we can do. Very ready to help, you know."

I let him rave on, digesting this information with a good deal of satisfaction and very mindful of all that Claire had said in the car coming home. I wondered whether to tell Byam of the ace which had been dealt or whether to save it and spring it on the meeting. This is what I decided to do.

As luck would have it, Hastings was away that day and,

mindful of the chaos in the drawing office, Byam and I decided to conduct the interview in Hastings' library. Heather stood by with the Sèvres cups and the silver coffee pot and Byam arranged that a number of files displaying the names of prestigious clients should be left carelessly lying about.

The front door bell rang and, giving her best imitation of an impeccably respectable and utterly faithful family retainer, Heather announced our visitors of which there were three. One seemed to be an architect who greeted us with false bonhomie. One was, I think, a quantity surveyor. One, I rather dreaded to suppose was a solicitor.

I think they were quite impressed by the elegance of the appointments and they may even have been impressed by the array of smart clients but I didn't think these things made them like us any the more. They didn't waste any time and after the briefest exchange of platitudes, they opened fire.

"It is our opinion that we have a very serious situation at Fitzclarence Street," they began.

I held up a hand. "Before we start talking about Fitzclarence Street," I said, "there's a minor and possibly totally irrelevant matter which it might be sensible to spend a few minutes discussing, if you don't mind."

They eyed me coldly. Byam eyed me with astonishment. I cleared my throat and soldiered on.

"You have a little job in Chelsea," I said. "Moore Street. I was there yesterday. We act for the adjoining owner Mrs. Phyllis Simpson. Curious co-incidence in a way - I understand your client is Sir James Ferguson's brother-in-law. As it happens, the adjoining owner is my aunt, so in a manner of speaking - ha, ha - you could say it's all in the family. You may not be aware of a rather serious situation which has arisen and extensive damage has been done to my client's property. Off the cuff yesterday, the contractors have - quite rightly - agreed to make good all the damage which has been sustained and, in the circumstances, we shall advise our client to take the matter no further, though, of course, there is the question of distress. She is an old lady living alone - heart condition, I believe - and walls collapsing around you, that sort of thing, can be distressful and alarming as I'm sure I don't need to tell you."

I was gratified by the effect of my words. I'm not actually sure that I've ever had a more satisfactory moment. They gaped. Byam gaped too.

I leaned forward and in confidential tones continued, "Of course, we'll keep a cover on this. I'm sure the last thing in the world Sir Hanbury would wish would be for this to become a news item... which it so easily could... and if we could come to some sort of accommodation in the matter of Fitzclarence Street, we'd be quite prepared to advise our client that she need distress herself no longer. We would have to confirm the matter with Sir Hastings who is the senior partner and I haven't had an opportunity to discuss the matter fully with Mr. Alexander, but I think I can say that we would be prepared to deal with the matter in that way."

Byam took up the running. "Coffee anybody?" he asked with a sunny smile. "Seems to be a bit left in the pot." And, as he whom I had identified as the solicitor fumbled in his pocket, "Do smoke if you want to - we don't usually in this room but if I just open the window a little bit - there - now what were we saying?"

There was a pause, a pretty long pause. I fished out a Gauloise, lit it and sat back.

"Are you offering us a deal?" one of them asked incredulously.

"Well, I don't know that I'd call it a deal exactly," I said. "A little accommodation..? It goes without saying that we would undertake on our client's behalf to make good any damage which it might be proven occurred to the Fitzclarence Club as a consequence of our operation, but obviously, in the meantime we would wish to proceed with the works which - as I am sure Mr. Alexander would agree

- you are absolutely free to inspect at any time."

"Yes, yes," said Byam.

"But would you like to talk this over amongst yourselves?"

"I don't think that'll be necessary," said the solicitor grimly. "This is precisely the kind of publicity that Sir Hanbury could do without at present. With his action against 'Private Eye' in the pipe-line and this Nolan business... and, confidentially, I understand he's the subject of some other disagreeable photographs which are going the rounds in Fleet Street. Sir James would not be pleased if we were instrumental in exposing his brother-in-law to the kind of publicity that you're hinting at."

There was a further pause at the conclusion of which Byam said enquiringly, "Deal?"

The architect spoke for the first time. "Deal," he said heavily.

XII

Casualty Kitchen.

When it comes to the design of kitchens I sometimes think it's me and the rest. I really am very good at it. I'm not only good but I can design a kitchen very quickly. Many architects will tell you that such a fiddling job can only be run at a loss. Not so at Spring House! We now have drawers full of details, folders full of materials and, in fact, have reached a stage where we can put together an elaborate set of drawings nearly all of which merely repeat something we have done before. I suppose this is rather a sneaky way of going about it but it really works extremely well.

We are not only good at designing kitchens, we are very knowledgeable on the subject of sinks, cookers, microwaves, dishwashers and the like and we know a great deal about materials. We used at one time to use teak extensively and then oak and for a while elm. Currently we are into ash, enjoying the straight grain and the pale cream colour. It looks very good with a dark tiled top. We make use of things like brass taps; we scorn melamine. Exotic terra cotta tiles are shipped to us from Italy and Portugal and slate floor coverings quarried anywhere from the Arctic circle to South Africa.

The latest kitchen was heralded by a detailed letter from a Mr. Marchant-Scott, writing from an address in Harley

Street. Putting two and two together we deduced that he was a surgeon. Reading his letter we gathered that he owned a weekend retreat on the Suffolk coast. Reading on, it emerged that he needed a new kitchen and finally there was a suggestion that I should meet him there the following Saturday.

It's no good. If you want to stay in business in this part of the world, you have to accept that many clients will be weekenders and Saturdays are constantly being requisitioned.

"Come on," Ron would say. "More days, more dollars."

I duly set off to meet the surgeon, his wife and his two children.

The house was two coastguard's cottages knocked together, knocked together as it happens by Charlie Boldero and not very skilfully either. I was later to discover that he'd got fed up with this client half way through the job and, with false bonhomie and seeming care, had modestly recommended Mr. Marchant-Scott to come to us to design his kitchen.

The surgeon was large and florid. He spoke precisely and very quietly. I felt that he had cultivated his hushed manner through years of breaking the news to patients and their relatives. His wife was mouse-like and hardly took any part in the ensuing conversation. It was clear from the outset that her views were not to be regarded and, indeed, he had a disconcerting, if not to say, appalling, habit of closing his eyes whenever she spoke and when she had finished, resuming at the point where he had broken off. I tried to draw her into the conversation; I tried to ask her what she thought; I tried to see if she had any sort of preference of any sort at all. I tried to enthuse her - "The kitchen's the woman's domain after all," I heard an oily voice which, with shame, I recognised as my own.

"I do most of the cooking at the weekends," said the surgeon in level tones and he went on to describe the

126

complicated systems he had evolved in doing anything from making a soufflée to boiling an egg.

His children were the neatest and most silent children I think I have ever met. Demurely they sat, listening to all that was said, until one of them moved, whereat Marchant-Scott said, "Go and play in the garden till lunch time." He didn't say, "Would you like to go and play in the garden?" He didn't say, "Are you bored? Why don't you go and play in the garden?" He just said, "Go and play in the garden." And, thereafter, they were to be seen running about dutifully and tidily in the achingly tidy garden.

I suppose in a way we had quite a productive conversation. We had at least established that he was seeking an island unit in the middle of the room on which most, if not all, the cooking would be done with a hi-tech extractor hood above it.

So detailed were the functional requirements that it wasn't until I got home that I realised that, amazingly, we had hardly discussed materials at all. I thought this wasn't a bad thing when I came to reflect and I decided that I would knock their eye out with a carefully prepared swatch of samples and glamorous photographs of things that we had achieved and, surprised not to be offered a drink at the end of the meeting, I made my way home in time for lunch.

A fortnight or so later, having prepared a bit of a presentation I went across to see them again. In the interval they had become Graham and Rosemary. The children were not introduced. With sunny confidence I produced my scheme and laid it on the table. I explained circulation, drew attention to the magical skill with which I had reduced movement to the bare minimum. I made play with my economical service layout; I indicated the skill with which morning sunlight would illuminate what Graham called 'the breakfast corner'. I even told them where, neatly, they could stack trays.

So far though I can't say that my offering was received with enthusiasm, at least it was received without dissent.

Drawing a deep breath I then began to talk about materials. Natural materials, rough textures, strong colours, a certain amount of whitewashed fair-faced brickwork and so on. To my chagrin, the expected round of applause did not materialise. Rosemary began to look uncomfortable; Graham fell even more silent.

"Kitchens become family rooms in no time," I said. "I tried to make it as much a sitting room as a work room. We don't want it, after all, to look like an operating theatre, do we? Ha, ha, ha!"

"Perhaps I should explain," said Graham coldly, "and I would have explained this earlier had I not thought it was absolutely obvious - an operating theatre is exactly what we do want. That is exactly what the kitchen is not only to look like but to be like."

"Graham and I met in an operating theatre," said Rosemary nervously. "I was theatre sister and he was the RSO, that's the Resident Surgical Officer. It was in Newcastle," she added. Characteristically Graham waited a second or two after she had finished speaking, added nothing to what she had just said and returned to the subject.

And so the conversation wore on to a conclusion until, insisting on going out into the garden to say goodbye to the children, (feeling that thereby I had scored a point of some sort, though I'm not quite sure what,) I returned to Spring House pretty fed up with Marchant-Scott and his kitchen.

I shared my troubles with Byam.

"Operating theatre, eh? You may be good at kitchens but perhaps you didn't know that I am pretty good at operating theatres. When I was with Travers Hayward, I practically did nothing else. I can't tell you how boring it was! I expect I've forgotten most of it but I can remember some nifty phrases... Shall I take this one over from you then you can get on with Wethersett Mill?"

I thought this was a good offer and Byam duly took over and the immaculate conception kitchen took shape on the drawing board, my layout, Marchant-Scott's hideous colour scheme and Byam and Kirsten's draughtsmanship.

"How did you get on with them?" I asked after Byam's first visit.

"Very well," he said. "Yes, it went very well. They said once more that they'd met in an operating theatre and I said, 'Trying to recreate and encapsulate the romantic atmosphere? Timing your heart beat by the time-elapsed clock? Checking the remaining kitchen towels against the swab-count panel? Holding hands in the shadow of the diathermy boom?'"

"What on earth's a diathermy boom?" I said.

"Not quite sure. I think it brings down a red hot needle and it cauterises things or people or whatever... I said all this to them and, if you can believe, Graham said in all seriousness, 'We shan't need a diathermy boom,' and I said, 'Why not? Could be a breakthrough - no kitchen complete without a diathermy boom - thread it through your kebabs et voilà - cook things from the inside out - no end to the possibilities.' He didn't think it was funny, in fact, it flashed through his mind that I might be approaching this major work in a spirit of frivolity."

In due course, the kitchen took shape and in due course it was finished. White work surfaces, white units finished in moulded plastic, stainless steel this, stainless steel that, white tiles from floor to ceiling, anti-static flooring - it didn't have the cosy Spring House look. Towards the closing stages there was a collision between Byam and Graham.

If you've got an island work unit you need a pretty efficient extractor hood. The extractor hood that Byam designed was about 6' by 3' bound in stainless steel, suspended by steel rods from the ceiling and packed with tubular lights.

"What's the distance," Graham asked, "between the work surface and the underside of the hood?"

Kirsten who happened to answer the telephone told him.

"Far too high," said Graham. "Far too high! Have you worked this out?"

"I'm sure Mr. Alexander and Mr. Simpson worked it out most carefully," said Kirsten, waggling her eyebrows at me. "Is it in question?"

"Well I don't know about that," said Graham. "Handed it over to the ventilating engineer at the hospital and he agrees with me. Far too high. Shouldn't be more than six hundred millimetres at the most... five hundred and fifty would be better."

"I will inform Mr. Alexander," said Kirsten in a voice frozen with chilly correctness.

When Byam came back she told him she had lowered his hood to six hundred millimetres.

"Far too low," said Byam firmly. "He'll have to get on hands and knees and get underneath it before he can see what he's cooking. He could singe his eyebrows! Still, his be the funeral." And we thought of other things.

Byam came back from the next inspection (the kitchen having been used for the first time over the weekend) in modest triumph.

"Hey Kirsten! Jack!" he said. "Something to tell you! Guess what! Graham's in hospital!"

"Well, he'd be likely to be in hospital," said Kirsten. "That's where he works. That's where he earns his living."

"No, no," said Byam, "you misunderstand me. He's in hospital as a customer."

"Why? What happened? Something suddenly snapped and Rosemary pinned him to the kitchen notice board with one of six matching Sabatier knives? Better still, did she shove the diathermy needle up his bum?"

"None of those things," said Byam, "but even better! He'd dressed himself up in a sort of chef's overall, assembled his materials round him and proceeded with the utmost parade to grill a fillet steak. (I'll bet those kids didn't get any of it.) And, guess what? He leans forward the better to observe its progress and hits himself smack dab between the eyes on the corner of the hood (which, if you remember, is about as yielding as the leading edge of a battle axe!) Laid his scalp open from chaps to chine! White extruded melamine surface drenched in gore, fillet steak sizzling in an exotic jus! Rosemary in her element, of course, clamping, staunching and swabbing! They carted him off to hospital. He's had ten stitches. Quite a scene, I think you'll agree. Never seen Rosemary in better form!"

"Yes," said Kirsten considering, "six hundred above the work surface - that would be just about skull height."

XIII

The Hard Sell.

Melbury Hall was, by any standards, a great big house. Founded in the 17th Century, it had so many 18th Century improvements that its romantic origins were lost to view and it now presented a run of nine neat sash windows within neat architraves, neat rustication, a classical pediment enclosing an armorial cartouche and a balustraded terrace.

It had housed morose Italian prisoners of war and had not been much improved by this. After the war, Sir Hastings was called in to put the house together again and to provide such things as bathrooms in which the house had been notably lacking. The owner, James Melbury, was an old mate of Hastings and over the following years they had together carried out a little improvement here, a little embellishment there and, from time to time a desperately needed repair.

When James Melbury died, Hastings, as an old family friend had continued to look after the house, acting now for the widowed Emma Melbury. Every now and then she would write to Hastings and tell him to send in an account. Every now and then, reluctantly, he did so and so the friendly connection between the firm and the house had continued through fifty years or thereabouts.

It wasn't the most money-spinning job we had ever had,

indeed, I dare say that in terms of strict accounting we just about broke even but there were many compensations. It was good to be associated with so many fine things. It was challenging to sort out the repairs as they fell due, in the most economic and satisfactory way. There gathered round us a team of builders and others who knew the house as we did and I don't suppose they made much money out of it either. You could always get a cup of tea or coffee - lunch from time to time - and at the end of most days, a pretty massive drink. Emma Melbury battled gallantly on to keep the roof on the house, the roofs on the many outbuildings, fill in the pot holes in the drive, rewire a bit from time to time and fund these operations by selling off a bit of land here and a bit of land there. In spite of these changes, and though by degrees the garden got smaller, any one of half a dozen generations of Melburys, returning, would have recognised the house as the house they had known, with its stabling, its garden houses and its chestnut avenue.

As Hastings increasingly withdrew, Melbury drifted into the care of Byam and myself. We became fond of the house; we became fond of Emma and twice voted her 'Client of the Year'. We had for some time been uneasily aware that the house was well overdue for external redecoration and extensive repair to the considerable acreage of stucco. We hated to mention these things; we knew Emma Melbury pretty well and had not even the remotest idea where she might raise the money for this large operation. We considered the possibility of grant but here encountered the inevitable anomaly that desperate repairs are often grant-aided but careful anticipatory husbandry is not. A stitch in time might save nine stitches but it didn't save anything else. ·

While we were pondering Emma's problems, she had a stroke of luck. Advised by Hastings in a percipient moment, she had applied for planning consent to extract gravel from a distant corner of the estate, and perhaps to our surprise, with success and in due course work began on the gravel pits and one began to visualise - at the end of it all - a chain of landscaped lakes. It wasn't, as such things go, a very extensive proposal but it was clear to us that it would fund the immediately necessary work and perhaps leave a bit in the pot for the future. Emboldened by this, we felt strong enough to break the news to Emma that she had a large job on her hands.

In spite of the inevitable diminishment in Emma Melbury's lifestyle over the years, she was still a pretty stylish lady. She was able to keep a horse, she was able to hunt occasionally. She drove a large, though rather ancient car. She continued to entertain. It was a confident image.

A confident image but, as such, she was vulnerable. Widow lady living alone in a large house, known to have had a windfall, she was a perpetual prey to roving salesmen (even to roving architects) who thought perhaps that her structural problems might present a profitable field. Perhaps it was lucky that she had us and our attendant squad of builders and she referred all such approaches and all such enquiries to us. Mostly we took no notice of them.

There came a day, though, when she rang to say, "Got a thing in the post today. Wondered if I ought to take it seriously. Do you know anything about a firm called 'Rockamadur'? They do a '... microporous' (whatever that may mean) 'resin-based wall coating containing a powerful algaecide' - non-toxic - as well, apparently... 'carrying a fifteen year guarantee if applied by one of our field teams of trained applicators'. Applicators!"

"Don't know anything about it," said Byam who had fielded this telephone call. "I'll find out if you like."

"Well," said Emma, "I must say I'm tempted. It might be the answer to my problems. They are quick - very quick. The whole job would be over in two days and I wouldn't have to go to the trouble of erecting scaffolding - they bring their own hoist with them apparently and spray the stuff on. They go on to say that they are 'targetting our area and can offer a discount of up to thirty percent of cost, to form part of a promotional programme to be run this spring. Thirty percent? I'm all for people offering me a discount of thirty percent. They may be the most terrible rogues but - I'll tell you what - this man (whose signature I can't read - it looks like Firework, but I don't think it can be) the regional manager, will, he tells me, be 'evaluating the sales potential' in 'this and adjoining hamlets on the 13th through 14th prox.' and thinks I might spare him some of my 'valuable time'. He's pretty sure that I won't regret this because, among other things, 'this sensational offer is not likely to be repeated'."

"What do you want me to do?" said Byam.

"Well, the trouble is, he rang up yesterday and although I didn't exactly mean to, I seem to have made an appointment for him to come here on Wednesday week to be targetted or assessed..."

"...or ripped off," Byam interpolated.

"Well, yes, very likely and I'd feel better if you could be there. Could you?"

Byam, of course, agreed.

On the the 14th prox. (though by then it was the 14th inst.) he duly set off to the Hall just before lunch to confront Mr. Firework in the company of Emma Melbury. He accepted a glass of sherry and read Mr. Firework's mail shot. Many glossy photographs of many stuccoed houses, all covered, no doubt, with Rockamadur's best, all looking very much the same, in various colours from ivory through to dark cream (other colours available by arrangement.) Mr. Firework - whose name turned out to be Fishlock - was modest, deferential and tremendously sincere. He blinked a little bit when Byam was introduced as Emma's architect but rallied and said, "So glad to have you in the line-up. As you and I well know, a job of this size - you can't afford to cut corners and we'll want to give Mrs. Melton the best advice - the very best advice."

Byam agreed.

He flipped his briefcase open to reveal a neat array of brochures, samples, electronic note-takers, a lap-top something or other with a discreetly winking light which emitted an occasional and confidential gurgle. Speaking rapidly and confidingly, Mr. Fishlock began to explain the virtues of Rockamadur. He told a few pointed anecdotes describing occasions when he had been lucky enough to prevent a client from taking 'an entirely wrong decision'. Turning to Byam he said, "And you and I recognise how easily mistakes can be made."

The room was warm, the sherry was good and Byam found himself nodding owlishly as the sales pitch unfolded and was only able to still the flood of information by producing a set of drawings. "We shall need an estimate," he said at last, repressively. "Here is a complete set of floor plans and elevations. You may like to take these away with you."

Mr. Fishlock allowed himself a deprecating, possibly even a pitying, laugh. "I shan't need to take these away," he said. "If I could just have a little walk round now I could come back to you and put the package in front of you."

Emma and Byam were left alone.

"Nice little man," said Emma.

"What a shit!" said Byam. They spoke with one breath.

"Oh, I don't think so," said Emma. "I thought he was rather nice. Certainly knows his stuff and thirty percent..."

"I would need to know thirty percent of what," said Byam.

In a surprisingly short time Mr. Fishlock returned and settled down. Flipping open his lap-top, he began to punch buttons. Byam and Emma sat in respectful silence, listening to clicks and bleeps. At the end of this period, Mr. Fishlock emerged with a smile.

"As near as I can make it," he said, "I'm saying 24K."

"Twenty four K?" Emma asked in puzzlement.

"Twenty four thousand," said Byam, "twenty four

thousand pounds."

"Is that with or without discount?" said Emma.

"Discount?" said Mr. Fishlock, momentarily puzzled.

"Yes," said Emma, "in your letter - I have it here - you said that you were offering a thirty percent discount and to quote you further, you said - 'Congratulations! You have been selected...' Well, what I want to know is - when does the discount get taken off?"

Mr. Fishlock's geniality suddenly seemed to wane. "Oh, that," he said. "Giving you a discount would entirely depend on whether you could manage to hit my time frame. At present we're working our way through your post code and we shall set up a series of back to back contracts, in fact the girls are out in the minivans knocking on doors already. It's a very rigid, computerised programme. The discount is only available if this can work within the established parameters timewise. We would need to load you on to the back of the previous job. And there are other advantages to proceeding with Rockamadur. We shall be bringing out new literature and, believe you me, we only touch prestige jobs. You would find yourself in the very best company, I promise you. Of course, we do expect any client in receipt of our generous discount to promulgate the virtues of the Rockamadur system within their postcode."

"What?" said Emma, startled. "Do you mean I should have to be open to the public?"

A deprecatory shake of the head appeared to deny this and Mr. Fishlock murmured something about photographic promotions and client endorsement listings.

"That's all fine," said Byam, "and I'm sure I'd be speaking for Mrs. Melbury if I said that we would be proud to be associated with such a get-up-and-go, up-to-the-minute concept but there is one formality and that is - I shall require a written estimate, detailing processes and procedures to say nothing of the materials on which this offer will depend, and setting out with precision the dates on which the offer will depend. Mrs. Melbury cannot necessarily hold herself available to be loaded onto the back of the previous job without a little notice."

Mr. Fishlock's geniality descended still further. "You're not, I hope expecting a competitive estimate? You might as well compare a Rolls Royce with a Ford Fiesta! Obviously, you can't begin to compare our state-of-the-art process with the finish you'd get from two plasterers with a ladder and a bucket. You only have to inspect the photographic evidence," he went on, passing a glossy brochure to Byam, "and, as you will see, we always roll the credits for the architect."

Byam began to turn the pages of the Rockamadur brochure while Mr. Fishlock droned on, idly at first but suddenly with attention. His eye focussed on a house called - as best I can remember - 'Russet Timbers'. He learned that it had recently 'benefited from the full Rockamadur treatment in the colour soft amber'. He further learned that the architect had been Thomas Boldero, Sons & Partners. Charlie's mob. On an impulse, Byam excused himself ('Important telephone call... quite forgot...') and slipped from the room.

"Charlie!" he said when he got to a telephone. "Tell me something quickly. Russet Timbers - house in Steeple Bancroft? You were the architect."

"Was I?" said Charlie. "If you say so but I don't remember anything about it."

"If I'm to believe what I see," said Byam, "you treated it externally with a Rockamadur finish. You must have heard of Rockamadur? 'Rockamadur - your finish for life!'"

"Oh, that!" said Charlie. "That's right... yeah... no, we had nothing to do with it. Where do you get all this from?"

"I'm reading a brochure issued by Rockamadur which illustrates the house and it says you were the architect. Come on, Charlie, wake up! You can't have forgotten."

Charlie exploded down the telephone, "I wasn't the bloody architect! I was called in to see what could be done after it had been treated by Rockamadur. Good God! They had problems - nine inch walls, no insulation, encased in concrete..."

"Concrete?"

"Well, call it Rockamadur if you like but it might just as well have been concrete. No, the place was wringing with condensation internally and I'll tell you something else about Rockamadur if you want to know - you can't get it off and it won't stay on. They described me as the architect did they? What a bloody cheek! Hey, tell you what - I'll sue! That's a good idea! Damages do you think? Wouldn't be surprised. Thanks for the tip, Byam."

"But what did your clients do?"

"They followed my advice. As you know clients don't always do that!"

"Which was what?"

"Sell the bloody place!"

Byam returned to the drawing room and to the company of Emma and Mr. Fishlock. Mr. Fishlock was expounding the advantages of entering the house for the Rockamadur house of the year competition, the winner of which would gain an all expenses paid two days at Eurodisney. He cut in. "Russet Timbers?" he said. "I've just been looking at your brochure..."

"Ah, yes, Russet Timbers. Little house in Essex. Well, we put that in to show that the treatment suits houses of all sizes. As you know, no order too big for Rockamadur but this is to show that no order's too small either. As we so often say - 'We're only there to help,' after all."

"I've just been talking to the architect," said Byam, "Boldero and Partners."

"Ah, yes," said Mr. Fishlock with only slightly diminished confidence, "old Charlie! Good friend of ours. What did he have to tell you?"

"Well, the brochure says that he specified Rockamadur high density, stress-graded finish in soft amber at Russet Timbers. I have to tell you, Mr. Fishlock, that he hotly denies the imputation. He thinks an action for libel would lie.

Coldly, Mr. Fishlock rose to his feet. "I'm not staying here to listen to this!" he said, snapping his briefcase shut and he stalked from the room.

"Libel?" said Emma. "What was that all about?"

"Charlie didn't want it supposed that he'd specified the wretched stuff. He's not the greatest architect in the world but he'd know better than to specify Rockamadur. On his advice, the owners have sold the house and lucky to do so since it appears to be encased in a thin film of concrete."

"Oh, Byam," murmured Emma, "where would I be without you?"

"Encased in concrete apparently!"

XIV

Ron's Revenge.

"What's the matter with you?" I said one day to Ron, finding him uncharacteristically sitting in his office staring into space.

"Bored!" he said even less characteristically. "Bored! Pissed off! All very well for you - I've been stuck in the office for weeks. Everybody else gets out and about while I sit here dealing with the nitty gritty."

I saw what he meant. It really did sometimes seem that Ron was consigned to the engine room below the water line while the rest of us paced the bridge in the fresh air. "I'm going to have a look at a little job this afternoon," I said. "Why don't you come with me? It's a little job at Markham Cross just south of Chelmsford. It's a nice day - a little run in the country will do you good and I could do with someone on the other end of the tape measure."

Ron ruminated. "Markham Cross...?" he said. "Reminds me of something or other... I can't remember what. Yer, no, I'll come with you. It'll make a change." He shouted, "Heather! I'm going over the border with Young Lord Lochinvar this afternoon. Field the telephone!"

We set off together. Always a pleasure to get out and about with Ron; escape from the office seemed always to release a rich vein of reminiscence and today was no exception. Each town we passed through triggered a memory of clients good or bad, jobs to be noted with satisfaction or skipped by with eyes averted.

Markham Cross when we got there turned out to be a smart dormitory, a satellite of Chelmsford, an expensive commuters' settlement. The houses were all shapes and sizes and of all periods but in some strange way they all looked the same. As we drove back and forth searching for our destination I decided that this was because they seemed to have matching cars; they seemed also all to patronise the same garden centre; sitting in neat front gardens they seemed even to have the same dog.

Ron's stream of reminiscence stilled for a moment. "What sort of job is this? Meant to ask you. What have we come to look at?"

I explained. "The railway station is closed," I said, "in fact the railway station is largely cleared away but what was the stationmaster's house remains. James Roberts - an old mate of mine from University - and in common with everybody else who lives in this place apparently, a merchant banker - has just bought it and he's asked me to check it over for him, look at the potential and come up with a few trendy ideas... you know the sort of thing... This outing has at least got this to be said for it - it oughtn't to be difficult to find the station!"

I was wrong. Turn as we might, explore one tree-lined avenue after another as we did, the station continued to elude us and at the end of a frustrated half hour when I was nervously convinced our details had been passed the breadth of the town on the Neighbourhood Watch tomtom, Ron spotted a discreet and faded sign - 'STATION LANE'. Station Lane may at some time have had a measure of Victorian dignity; it was now little more than a muddy lane between the fences of two not particularly pretentious houses. We nosed our way dubiously along this unpromising thoroughfare which, after a hundred yards or so, turned sharply to the right and revealed the Station Master's House.

The station had, indeed, disappeared and consequently the little house seemed sadly truncated. It had, however, a good deal of architectural pretension. Surprisingly it was built of carstone, a strange ginger coloured stone that hitherto I had only seen in north Norfolk. As a concession to local product this odd ginger coloured material was enlivened with snow white brick dressings. Its gables - of which there were a large number - were decorated with terracotta finials. Its front door which was massive had a faintly Gothic flavour and was embellished with large square-headed iron nails.

I thought it was delightful, like a toy house. Ron thought it was appalling. "What a tip!" he said disparagingly as we sat in the car contemplating our immediate professional future. "This bloke of yours," he said, "merchant banker didn't you say? Well he can afford something a bit better than this surely?"

"Oh, come on Ron," I said. "It's trendy. It's different. It's your artisan chic. It'll be in all the glossies, you watch."

"Yer," said Ron, "an' I expect an old ghost train'll come through every night at midnight! '...if it be a natural thing - where do it come from? Where do it go?...'"

We unlocked the massive front door and made our way inside. It was, I must say, a very odd house. There seemed to be an enormous number of rooms, all very small. Every single one had a fireplace (which accounted for no fewer than five twisted chimney stacks.) The staircase was narrow and steep, the bedrooms, all of which had partly sloping ceilings, were not much more than adequately illuminated by tiny dormer windows. There was a fine cast iron range in the kitchen and this did cheer Ron up for a moment. "Cakebread, Robey," he said, reading the manufacturer's name cast in its top. "Good old firm they were," and he proceeded in a knowing way to explain how you controlled the draught and what most of the knobs, levers and slides were supposed to contribute to the comfort of a line of bygone stationmasters.

We got a tape out and whipped round the house together at practised speed, hardly pausing to look about us and very soon we had finished.

"Two hours and ten minutes," said Ron with satisfaction, looking at his watch. "I bet not many could survey a four bedroomed house in two hours and ten minutes! Remind me to charge your friend five hours - he won't know any different."

"I was thinking of eight hours," I said.

Thoughtfully, I had provided a thermos of coffee and thoughtfully the last stationmaster had left a small table, a battered arm chair and a stool behind him.

"I don't know what it is," said Ron, "but I can't escape the feeling that I've been here before you know - not in this house but in this village. Now, I wonder what...? There's something there..."

Hardly thinking what he was doing, he set down his coffee mug and began to examine the built in kitchen dresser. "What will he do with all this brown paint?" he said disparagingly, running a finger over the surface.

"It's not just old brown paint," I said. "It's grained, subtle, the original thing. You'd pay a lot to recreate that finish these days. If you could find anyone who can do it."

"Humph! My uncle Jack used to do it with a comb!"

He continued his exploration of the dresser drawers, tugging at one which had got stuck.

"Hallo! This is a bit more interesting!"

He eased out of the drawer a wad of old newspaper cuttings which had been making it stick and followed this with a handful of yellow and crumbling, blotched and sepia-tinted photographs. He spread them gently out on the table top. They seemed to be views of Essex villages, some from the Twenties, one or two of them from before the First War.

"Could be worth a bit," muttered Ron. "Better keep them and give them to your chum. He can frame them and hang them in the hall... He's probably paid for them if you think about it...".

We turned them over together.

"Ah," he said. "Here we are - this must be Markham Cross station in its heyday... and there's the stationmaster in his heyday... three humble porters in tow - those were the days! And look, here's the High Street." He looked at the back. "1924." He looked at another. "Jubilee Avenue, 1924. Jubilee Avenue? Jubilee Avenue, Markham Cross?... I don't know!" He stared with concentration at the photograph.

We packed our things up, placing the photographs carefully in my briefcase and locked the door behind us, Ron still in the grip of his unaccustomed abstraction. He sat silent as we turned into the High Street, looking about him then, abruptly said, "Take the next right down here, Jack, will you? Why don't we have a quick look at Jubilee Avenue? See what's changed?"

I turned into a street of unremarkable buildings, most Victorian in origin judging by their first floors where there were some pretty details still evident over the ground floor ranks of shops of a later date. Ron began to get excited as we passed the window of number ten where a single swathe of provençal fabric, elegantly illuminated, announced the design services of 'Lis Oulivado'.

"Go slowly, Jack, past number 6. Next to the Estate Agency, just before Posh Paws Poodle Parlour. What is it?"

We peered at the blacked-in shop front almost invisible in the rank of glittering frontages and I read out the elegant gold lettered sign which said, 'A. PRICE & SON. PERSONAL FINANCE ARRANGERS. DISCRETION GUARANTEED.'

"Hah!" Ron exclaimed with satisfaction, "So that's it! Okay, Jack, I've seen enough. Off we go."

He relapsed into silence again on the way back to Spring House and when we got out, with a laconic - 'Just going up to check something in the loft' - he disappeared up the stairs.

Mystified by this, I reported to Kirsten and Byam, had a

cup of tea with Heather and was just preparing to go home when Ron descended. "Come here," he said, "and have a look at this! I'll tell you something - you know I've been nagging on about Markham Cross? Well it wasn't called Markham Cross in the old days - it was Markham Halt. Not smart enough I suppose - they changed its name and that's what confused me. Well I've remembered! In '47, 48 maybe - just after the war - I did a war damage job in Jubilee Avenue. They'd dropped a couple of bombs. About nine houses were damaged, four of them knocked out completely. Well I had a client who owned number six. Let me show you something..."

He produced a dog-eared drawing, rough and untidy by the standards of the present day but, nevertheless, clearly from the hand of the youthful Ron Steel. "I did his war damage claim for him. Forgotten about it until this morning. I rebuilt number six. Now this is the point. What you did in those days was a notional identical reinstatement. Of course, no drawings available, no nothing of what was there before except maybe the foundations. So what did we do? Guessed what it must have looked like from the ones that remained. You put your drawing together, waved it at the War Department Damage Assessor, argued the toss and in the end agreed a price. What a caper it was! Timber rationed, every bloody thing rationed! Building licences! Oh, you don't know you're half alive! Anyway, I rebuilt number six."

"Well good for you Ron," I said. "First job?"

"Yep," said Ron, "my first job. And there it is to this day. But that's not the point. Now look at the drawing again. Fixed in the mind? Okay? Have a look at this photo." And he produced the photograph of Jubilee Avenue circa 1924.

"Well, Ron, it looks to me as if you made a fair shot of guessing what it used to look like."

"You're half blind," said Ron, disparagingly. "Look again."

I looked again and ran my finger along the row of shabby

houses. Numbers 2, 4, 6, 8, 10 on that side of the street... but - wait a minute!... 2, 4 - 6? 2 and 4 in turn basement, ground floor, first floor and attic floor. Number 6 had basement, ground floor, first floor and a roof. No top storey!

"What are you telling me Ron?"

"What I'm telling you," said Ron, "is that, before it was hit by a bomb, number 6 was on three floors and when I'd finished with it it had four. Didn't know it at the time. At the time I suppose nobody knew it - nobody, that is, except for my client who had been running his business from there before the bomb dropped and who, you might have thought would have spoken up - Mr. A. Price."

"What? The same Price who's still there?"

"Must be."

"Well I hope your client was undyingly grateful for the extra floor you provided for him?"

Ron gave a wolfish grin. "Not he! Not Arnie Price! He was the neighbourhood money lender and pawnbroker in those days... mean as cat's meat. The bugger never paid my bill. Cute as a shit-house rat! Do you know - he rumbled the fact that I described myself as an architect. I wasn't an architect in those days and he could have caused me a lot of trouble... I was young and when you're young, you scare easy. I tried to have a go at him but I had to let it go in the end."

"You ought to have told Hastings," I said. "He'd have gone into action on your account."

"Didn't quite like to," said Ron. "I'd done the job in office time, hadn't I? On office paper. Of course, I don't think Hastings would have given a damn but I didn't know him all that well in those days. But there's unfinished business between me and Mr. Price. Yer, unfinished business..."

A few days later I heard Ron talking to Charlie Boldero on the telephone and a few days after that he came into the office bursting with pride.

"What do you think of this?" he said and laid a letter in

front of me. It appeared to be from The War Damage Commission.

"War Damage Commission?" I said. "But they were wound up years ago."

"Not everybody knows that," said Ron. "Read on!"

It was, indeed, from a person describing himself as B.W.Alexander, Senior Assessor at an improbable London City address, (Head Office), in spite of which, mystifyingly, it had the Spring House telephone number, (Regional Office). It told Mr. A. Price in measured tones that it had come to the attention of the Commission that, whereas, prior to the incident on the night of February the 14th 1942, number 6 Jubilee Avenue, Markham Cross had consisted of three storeys with basement, assisted by grant from the commission it had been rebuilt as four storeys with basement, that copies of photographs illustrating this were enclosed herewith. The thoughtful Mr. Alexander went on to say that an assessment of the overpayment had been made with due allowance for inflation and interest over the intervening fifty five years and if his cheque in the sum of £27,136.85 was received by the Commission within the ensuing 14 days, the Commission would probably waive their right to an action for fraud. He added that if Mr. Price wished to discuss the matter, perhaps he would he be so kind as to telephone the undersigned when arrangements would be made for him to explain his position at the next meeting of the Tribunal which would be at a not very distant date.

"Ron!" I said. "This is brilliant! How the hell did you do it? Where did this letterhead come from?"

"I put it together on Charlie Boldero's computer - he's got a colour printer, choice of fonts, the lot. With all these references I think it looks quite real, and it even printed it for me on this cheap and horrible paper these government departments usually use. I'll get Mr. A. to sign this and brief him - and Heather too - on what to say when Arnie Price rings up. As ring he will."

I found that I was disturbed by the confident and vindictive gleam in Ron's eye. "Poor old sod! He's probably ninety three by now! You're likely to give him a heart attack!"

"You're just beginning to get the idea," said Ron. "Tell you what - at the end of the day when all is revealed, I'll present him with an account for my fees again."

"Can you remember how much it was, Ron?"

"Only too clearly. It was £75."

I was still a little uneasy about Ron's scheme. "Look, Ron," I persisted, "what makes you so sure he's still living at number six? It's been a long while... and if he is still compos mentis he might not have have that kind of money - the £75, I mean, never mind the twenty seven thousand."

"Oh, he's there all right," said Ron with satisfaction. "I went back there didn't I? The next day. To the discreet little premises where he's still operating with his son Joey. Nothing changes does it? When I knew him Arnie was screwing cash out of the poor. Now he's screwing cash out of the not quite so poor - housewives who've spent too much on their credit cards and need to pay it off before their husband finds out, kids who just can't manage that last payment on the motor bike, family men who've been made redundant and need something to tide them over Christmas. Personal financial discreetly arranged, huh! 'Hand over your family allowance book, madam, and we'll see what we can do.' With the rates of interest he charges, they're in his pocket for life."

"How do you know all this, Ron?"

"Went in as a customer. Spun 'em a tale. Said I'd be in touch later. And I will!"

"But what happens," I said, "if he writes to this phoney address of yours, gets it back -'not known at this address'?"

"He won't," said Ron confidently. "I know what he'll do. He'll pick up the phone."

"Well then, hadn't you better tell Mr.A. what it's all about?"

We duly went to confer with Byam.

"You've got a new job," said Ron. "You're the Senior War Damage Assessor!"

"Anything you say Ron," said Byam equably. "What's all this about?"

And Ron explained.

"...so when this bloke rings up a Mr. B.W.Alexander will answer."

"No problems so far," said Byam.

"You tell him we're going to throw the book at him. Tell him - oh, tell him anything you like! Just put the frighteners on him. You can do it!"

I could see that Byam was viewing this with considerable relish; it was, after all just his sort of thing. He was very ready to produce a new persona to fit the new situation and I heard him at odd moments in the afternoon practising a senior bureaucrat, loss adjuster voice, confident, conceited and slightly bored.

The next morning there was a menacing phone call from a Mr. Joseph Price. We all heard Heather receive it and we all heard her say in a glacial and disinterested tone, "Mr. Alexander is in conference." And in reply to his next question, "There's nothing in his book at three o'clock this afternoon Mr. Price. You might be able to contact him then. May I tell him what this is about?.... And do you have a reference number?... I'll see that Mr. Alexander gets your message." And she rang off in considerable glee.

"Three o'clock," we all said in chorus. I was determined to be there.

Sure enough at three o'clock the telephone rang again and we heard Heather say, "Mr. Alexander? I'll try his line for you Mr. Price."

"We're off!" said Byam in a whisper and, out loud, "Alexander here. Mr? Yes, Mr. Price. What does this concern? You have a file reference number? Ah, yes, Jubilee Avenue, Markham Cross. What's your query Mr. Price?"

And the explosive voice of Joseph Price boomed out, "You don't suppose I'm going to pay this!!!!! Twenty seven thousand quid!!! You must be nuts!! Christ Almighty, this is bloody fifty years ago!! I'm not going to pay this! And anyway - where's the info come from?"

"It's quite a straightforward case, I think, Mr. Price," said Byam in a neutral tone. "We're only seeking reimbursement of the overpayment and the amount in question can be quite simply calculated. If you have anything you wish to say, it's open to you to appear before the Tribunal, or get your solicitor to come before the Tribunal if you prefer. The next date is the 15th of February, 10.30 at the Mansion House."

"The Mansion House?" said Joseph Price, clearly somewhat awed.

"Alternatively you could make a written submission..."

"But fifty years!" said Joseph Price. "You can't be serious!"

Byam allowed a note of menace to creep into his voice, "There is no statute of limitations where fraud cases are concerned, Mr. Price. It's our experience that these things very seldom come to court. It's open to you to take whichever course you wish but the facts are not in dispute and though it's no part of my job to advise you as to how you should proceed, the Tribunal has very wide powers."

"You're seriously telling me that I've got to write a bleeding cheque for twenty seven thousand pounds?" said Joey Price.

"That's what it comes down to Mr. Price," said Byam. "I mean - you're not disputing the facts, I have them all before me, let's see now... construction costs - £3,000, architect's fees £75... I see from the file that you were reimbursed for the architect's fees..." he paused and when no denial came carried on, "and, of course, the sum owing has been arrived at by consulting the current market value of the proportion of overbuild as calculated according to percentage of total floor area. We have a scale on which these things are worked out. Provided all goes smoothly, the Commission are not unreasonable... they will allow you fourteen days in which to pay. If you would like to make instalment payments we could probably come to some such arrangement. I must remind you that we are discussing a matter of fraud. All right?"

And, to Heather over his shoulder, "Who? Oh, fine, show him in, I shan't be a minute," and then back to Mr. Price, "I think that's all Mr. Price. Perhaps you'd let me know whether you will be at the Tribunal hearing? There's not a heavy agenda; it shouldn't take up more than six hours at the most and I can tell you that we have all the papers here."

Byam laid the telephone down carefully. "Shit scared!" he said with satisfaction. "Quaking with terror! Wonderful! Wonderful!"

"What happens next?" I asked.

"We let him sweat for a few days," said Ron, "then I take him on a little trip down Memory Lane. 'Remember me?' I'll say. 'Remember my little account for £75? £75 that you stuck in your back pocket and never paid out?' That money meant a lot to me in those days. It would have made all the difference at the time. I was counting on it. I had spent it even. And he had the bloody sauce to pocket it! Probably faked a receipt for it if I know him!"

"What do you reckon he owes you now Ron?"

Ron produced a calculation. "Eight hundred and thirty five pounds and seventy eight pence," he said. "Up to last Friday. It's all here."

And it was.

A few days later the phone rang and Heather appeared in the door with her hand over the receiver. "It's Mr. Price senior!" she said. "Wants to speak to Mr. Alexander. I said he wasn't here but he won't believe me."

"Mr. Price senior?" said Ron. "Old Arnie himself! Put him on!"

Switching the speaker through to conference he took the

telephone.

"Hello Mr. Alexander," said a husky and feeble voice. "It's Mr. Price senior speaking. I'm very shocked by all that has been said to my son. I can't believe you're going to take this matter up in this way. I'm ninety two! I haven't been well." A few dry coughs illustrated this. "I'm in a very small line of business here... don't have this sort of money... bidding fair to turn me out of the business I've given the whole of my life to building up. It wouldn't look too good if the papers got hold of this if you take my meaning..." The pathetic voice took on an overtone of slight menace, "... threatening a disabled old age pensioner..."

Ron made no reply and a silence fell. After a while Arnie Price said nervously, "Hello?"

"Hello Arnie," said Ron in boisterous tones. "Nice to hear you Arnie. Seems like a long time. Know the voice do you? No? Sorry to hear you're having a bit of bother Arnie. Not a lot I can do to help I'm afraid."

Arnie Price's voice which had been reedy and bronchitic suddenly strengthened. "Who's that?" he asked truculently.

"Well, top of the morning to you Arnie! It's Ron Steel."

If Arnie Price had been Macbeth at the appearance of Banquo's ghost, he could not have sounded more horror-stricken. "Ron Steel?" he breathed. "Ron Steel!"

"Listen to me Arnie," said Ron. "Fifty years ago you swindled me out of seventy five quid. Do you remember? Course you do! Seventy five quid may not seem like much but it bloody nearly sunk me at the time."

"You bugger!" said Arnie. "You've shopped me to the bleedin' Commission!"

"I haven't," said Ron, "but I could. I've got drawings, I've got photographs - it's all here. I could send it to the S.F.O. Tell you something Arnie. I'm a nice bloke - I like everybody to be happy. I'll make a deal with you. Pay my bill with interest - five percent compound over fifty years and I won't take the matter any further. Eight hundred and thirty five pounds and thirty eight pence - that's what you owe me. Stick a cheque for that amount in the post and send it to Spring House, Lavenham and you may hear no more but..."

"But," spluttered Arnie, "the War Damage Commission - you've set them on me!"

"I don't know how well you remember me Arnie but I was always just a bundle of fun, anything for a laugh - just thought I'd put the frighteners on you. War Damage Commission - nothing! Wound up years ago! The Serious Fraud Office still exists though and I could send the papers to them."

"This is bloody blackmail," said Arnie desperately.

"Well Arnie," said Ron, "you may be ninety two or whatever you are but you're not thick! Seems like you've got the idea."

"The S.F.O. will never touch it after this length of time," said Arnie.

"Like to find out, would you?" said Ron. "Tell you what - I'll send you an up to date invoice to account rendered 14th March 1947 and all that. It'll be very nice hearing from you again!"

He rang off and sat back. "Got 'im!" he said. "After all these years! Got 'im!"

XV

Style Wars.

"Do you know what happened to dinosaurs?" Sir Hastings enquired one day, looking up from a letter over which he had been clicking and tutting with disapproval for ten minutes. "I mean - how they became extinct? Pretty impressive in their day, dinosaurs, you know. Where are they now?"

"I always understood that their eggs got eaten up by lively and tactically-minded mammals - our ancestors that is," Kirsten suggested.

"No such thing," I said. "They got wiped out when an asteroid fell on Mexico. The sunlight got blotted out for decades by the layer of sulphuric dust it kicked up and that was the end of them."

"No, no," said Byam. "They met every threat to their lifestyle by growing another layer of armour plate until they were so heavy they could hardly move and they either sank with a gurgle to the bottom of a Jurassic Swamp or they fell victim to more agile adversaries who'd had the sense to stay out of the specialisation game."

"Yes," said Sir Hastings, "all those things. But especially the last. And I'll tell you - what happened to them is going to happen to us! Happen to architects, I mean. Architects today are so terrified of being sued for negligence they armour themselves against attack by writing ever more involved specifications, producing more elaborate drawings, surrounding themselves with consultants. I'm told there's a thing called Quality Assurance! Stuff and nonsense! Come back Sir Christopher Wren! The cost of their services goes through the roof, and suddenly they wake up one day and find they've made themselves redundant. And the last we see of them is the bursting of a nitrogenous bubble on the surface of the marsh and that is all to mark the passing of a once noble profession."

We contemplated this dire prophecy in silence for a moment.

"Nonsense, Uncle!" said Kirsten. "How you do go on!"

"Not nonsense, you know. Hardly design anything anymore."

"We do, you know," I said.

"Well, perhaps we do," said Hastings. "Last firm of architects left in England I sometimes think. Half the architects practising now never wield a pencil. Probably haven't got a pencil. Why bother with one when you've got computer aided design? Now, I tell you, if ever I see a picture of a stegosaur I say, 'Pass friend. I understand your problem.' Specialisation - that's what's going to finish us off. Here we sit doing a bit of this and doing a bit of that, doing anything that's put in front of us but that's because we're obsolete. I mean look at this job," he waved the letter he had just received, in front of us. "Will we take on the conversion of that terrible holiday camp between Harwich and Felixstowe to a 'Leisure Complex'? Leisure Complex indeed! And this is the cast list - we're supposed to be the architects, an outfit called Leisurehome are on board to 'manage'. What else have they got? Structural engineer, interior decorator, landscape architect, there's even a chap here specifically engaged to 'monitor environmental sensitivity'! See what I mean? What's left for us? Practically nothing. There's even an acoustic engineer and I suppose somewhere, toiling away below the waterline, there has to be a quantity surveyor - these are the furry little animals eating up our eggs.

"Used not to be like that. Chaps used to come along and give you a job and you got on with it. When I was a boy, architects were expected to do everything and they did. Dammit, I once designed a mayoral chain and the Town Hall to go round it. Town Hall was all right but the mayoral chain was hideous... Still, no worse than the things that get themselves designed by 'Civic Pride Accoutrement Design Services' if they exist and I expect they do. I don't know... time I was dead, I think."

"What are you going to do about this job, though?" said Byam.

"Turn it down. Turn it down. Can't get involved with all that rubbish! It would drive me absolutely crazy! Drive you fellers crazy too, come to that."

A few days later Hastings' stance in the matter was to be tested again. It was, at that period, impossible to open a glossy magazine without seeing a sumptuous interior from the hand of Adam Burbank who, it appeared, sat at the apex of the interior decorating business. He was an American with an international reputation. After a spectacular career from Beverly Hills to Gramercy Park, a career in which he had left a trail of uncomfortable and challenging interiors behind him and which had culminated in the appearance of his austerely handsome features on the cover of 'Time' magazine, he had declared himself bored with American culture. Exhausted by the attempt to convert the ladies of Washington from minimalism to the Gothic Revival, he had upped sticks and come to find his roots or the refreshing Spring of Creativity or something of that nature (I had all this from Claire who was translating it all from Paris Match) in Europe and, more precisely, in the Suffolk from which his mother's family had set sail in the Mayflower.

We had had an enquiry from Adam Burbank. I suppose we ought to have been flattered; in fact I will confess that I was flattered. A bachelor, he had bought a moated house of considerable splendour in the county and was proposing to do it up in his very recognisable style. He needed an architect to take care of the things architects are left to take care of - the drains, the down pipe runs, minor repairs here and there and, of course, materialising the lavish Burbank design schemes on site. It was a house on which we had worked in the past and had been, for a time, the property of one Billy Starr the pop singer whose frantic life-style had reduced him to a state of such physical collapse and whose successful career had filled his pockets with so much money that he had now decided to take his battered body and his bulging bank account into tax exile in Spain.

Byam persuaded Hastings to take the job on. "Damn it all," he said, "we know the house inside out - we've got a very good set of drawings. This Adam Burbank may be a royal pain - I hear he can be hell - but it could be a good job."

"Don't rush in there," said Hastings. "It's never easy, doing a job for another professional and from all we hear, this designer chap's likely to be a bit demanding. See what you can find out about him."

The first thing we found out about him was that he was a fiend. Byam had phoned around and tracked down a job he had had done for a film producer in Essex. The architect who had worked with him on the scheme was Charlie Boldero.

"Think of Everard McBride," said Byam, "and double it! I was talking to Charlie and, you know Charlie - affability itself - wouldn't harm a fly..."

"Terrible architect, all the same," I said.

"I dare say but this Burbank reduced him to a gibbering wreck. Endless meetings, endless changes of instructions, fearful scenes on site. There was a passage 900 mm wide on the drawings - 'Make it 3'6"' says Burbank, so they made it 3'6". 'Knock the partition down and make it 3'9"' says Burbank, so they made it 3'9" and, if you can believe, ten minutes later they made it 4'. The final account arrives, the contractor charges for rebuilding the partition three times. 'Not going to pay for that!' says Burbank with the magically seductive suggestion that poor old Charlie should pay for it on the grounds that they were rectifying a design fault! Poor old sod! His wife says he lost a stone and he used to wake up in the middle of the night - dictating letters in his sleep, he was."

"I bet it was Charlie's fault," I said unsympathetically. "You know what he's like! Never puts anything in writing... Doesn't surprise me that this Burbank got a bit fed up with him."

Uncharacteristically, therefore, Byam had decided in favour of letting this job go by. I was in favour of taking it on and that is what we did.

We were a only week into the contract before I began to feel that Byam had been right. First impressions had been rather favourable - Burbank was smooth, confident and supple. He was a good-looking man in his mid fifties, fit and tanned with impeccably cut dark hair just greying a discreet amount over his ears. He looked, in fact, as though he had been designed by himself. He had made the job sound very attractive - "My showcase but also and more importantly my home, Jack," he had said in tones of deep sincerity. "I see this project as a challenge to both our skills - retapage and maquillage in equal measure. Will you accept the challenge?"

"Oh, yes, um, count me in Mr. Burbank, er, Adam."

And our mission impossible began. The moment we got down to work I realised that he was indeed a bully. He had an appalling habit of arriving at Spring House, parking his car on the pavement and blowing his horn until one of us went down. He would then roll down the window and dictate about ten pages of notes. I tried to make him come in but he never had time and the best I could do was carry my notes back to the office, try to decipher them - not always easy since they had been scribbled with freezing fingers and occasionally in the rain - and try to put together a reasonable schedule of his amended requirements. I had to concede, however, that he really knew his stuff. He crackled with ideas and his touch was sure. Grudgingly I found myself approving his schemes and listening carefully as he explained his methods instead of waiting impatiently for him to finish. I learned about scumbling and craquelure or was it craquelage? Faux marbre and faux bois? I became expert. I learned that to create drama you emptied a room of furniture save for one interesting piece and painted the walls in sang de boeuf. If you then added dark green curtains in heavy silk you had a room to knock your eye out. I began to see where his fame had come from and if it hadn't been for his bad manners I would even have begun to enjoy the job.

In due course tenders were received and were not far off our forecast. Of the three contractors concerned, the job went to the one - how often this happens - to the one I would not have chosen. They were a good old-fashioned outfit but the management had just changed and, booted into the managerial chair was an eager but not very experienced and rather nervous youth called Gary Kenton who was to run the job from the builders' end.

At length - at considerable length - the contract started on site. Until now I had been the principal target of Burbank's venom. ('You shouldn't let him get away with it. You should be more firm,' Kirsten who was not involved in the job said very reprovingly from time to time.) But now the unfortunate Gary began to discover what life with Burbank was like. "How did he get my home telephone number?" he said to me desperately one day. "Eleven o'clock last night! And half past seven this morning! And that's not the worst of it! He comes strolling on site in his Gucci loafers and talks to the blokes. 'Is that the best you can do?' he said the other day. 'Hasn't Mr. Simpson explained that we want the best standard?' And you should have heard the screams and yells when he got the écru paint on his mohair suit! Never heard language like it! I tell you - the lads were all but ready to chuck their hand in last week. And I can't say I'd blame them! Raging poofter! He's got right up their noses!"

"So long as it's only their noses, Gary," I heard myself saying unguardedly.

And Burbank would turn to me and say, "Can't you find anyone better than those oafs you've brought on site? What's the matter with those guys? They don't seem to understand a word I say! They just stand there looking sulky!"

Stung at last by this I said, "This is Suffolk, Adam. This is the best team in Suffolk which probably means you've got the best craftsmen in the country. You may be able to get away with treating your work force like that in New York but you can't get away with it here. They're not used to it. You don't do yourself a favour. You want to congratulate them occasionally, give some sign that you appreciate what's going on... that's the way it goes down here."

Burbank exploded. "But I don't bloody appreciate what's going on! I think it's terrible! I think we're going to have to get another contractor."

"Cost you if you do," I said.

"Cost me? Cost me nothing! Who's responsible for monitoring the standard of work? You are! Isn't that the architect's job? I tell you what I want and you see I get it!"

And so this unproductive and deeply depressing conversation rolled on.

Gary and I both foresaw trouble in store when it came to the final account. Burbank's often repeated, 'I'm not going to pay for that!' rang constantly in our ears and I was more than usually particular to confirm every single thing he said in writing with copies to everybody in sight.

There came, however, a moment of respite. He was to be away for a fortnight. "Thank God for that!" I said. The contractor shook his head,

"Oh, I don't know... I'd sooner have the bugger where I can see him. Do a fortnight's work when he hasn't been here and I know what it'll be - 'That wasn't what I wanted! Don't you ever listen?' You mark my words, Jack, there'll be trouble when he gets back."

I had, of course, been equipped by Burbank with fax and telephone numbers and addresses scattered across the Balkans where the prospect of redecorating and reanimating two somewhat damaged British Embassies had led him.

"You never know your luck," said Ron. "Perhaps he'll get shot."

"You never know your luck," said Byam. "Confronted by the spectacle of human suffering, he may come back a changed, sadder, wiser and gentler man."

"Of course! How silly of me not to think of it! That's exactly what will happen."

What actually happened was that suddenly the spate of faxed instructions from Sofia, Zagreb, Sarajevo, Belgrade dried up and then there was a message saying his return would be delayed by a fortnight. Overall, he would have been away for a month. It came to us that we could well have finished the job by the time he got back. Gary had by now pretty well sunk into a trance of catatonic terror and didn't see this as a cause for rejoicing. He even went into a strident imitation of Adam - "'Call that finished?'" he shrilled. "I can hear it all!" and he tottered home for a cup of tea, a couple of tranquillisers and an evening spent frantically writing out lists of figures with a view to putting together a final account.

The month stretched to five weeks and finally a short fax from Adam informed us that he would be back after the weekend. The work was complete and on Saturday I went over with Gary Kenton to walk round the job, to check and admire now that the last ladder and bucket had been removed. I could see that it was pretty good. I could see that in the one or two places where I had deliberately ignored Adam's instructions I had pursued a wiser course. I could see that the panelling in what was known as the Big Room had been expertly scumbled and that the glaze gave it an impression of timeless magnificence. The question was, would Adam see it?

"I dunno..." said Gary appearing behind me. "One of the blokes said it looks as if somebody'd been sick on it... What do you think, Jack?"

I looked at it critically. It crept into my mind that it did look as if somebody'd been sick on it. "For goodness' sake, Gary, you're getting me as bad as you! Just get it into your nut that there's nothing wrong with this job!"

In no way cheered by my bracing remarks, he went with drooping shoulders on his way and left me to perambulate the attic bedrooms by myself. No problems there that I could see. I made a few notes. At length, reasonably satisfied with the result of my inspection, it being a fine day, I opened an attic dormer, leant my elbows in the sunshine on the windowsill and in the company of cooing pigeons, lit up a Gauloise. As I looked, a dark grey Saab came down the drive. I eyed it absently, subconsciously registering the fact that it was just like Adam's car. Just like Adam's car but it couldn't be his because there was a female at the wheel.

I hurried down, prepared if necessary to repel boarders. The job had aroused a good deal of interest one way and another and there had been a procession of inquisitive people peering through windows and even strolling in through the door. Gary Kenton had left the keys with me.

When I reached the ground floor the mystery occupants of the car were still in the car. Why were they still in the car? Because they were admiring the house? No. They were still in the car because they were locked in what, even through steamed up windows, I could see was a succulent embrace. I prepared a speech. "Pardon me, Sir and Madam," I planned to say, "we prefer to keep the front of the house clear of parked vehicles and direct those of amorous intent to the shrubbery where you will find every convenience including privacy."

I thought that would be pretty funny but the speech was never delivered. As I bore down on the car, in a tinkle of giggles, the driver's door opened and out stepped a bosomy blonde girl. She was wearing something soft, clinging and very short in pale blue. I guessed her age to be not quite thirty. At the same time the passenger's door crashed open and a figure in jeans and a suede jacket jumped out.

"Funny," I thought. "Car looks like Adam's. This bloke looks like Adam..."

There was a reason. It was Adam. Staggered by this turn of events - he wasn't after all due for another two days - I shrank back into the house, followed by cheerful voices. A bell-like, mittel-European soprano and the gravelly tones of Adam. I shrank further into the shadows.

"Hey, look at that panelling, Anastasia! Just look at that panelling! That's just the way I wanted it to be. Still, these are the best guys in Suffolk which means, I guess, the best in the whole country."

The situation was getting more surreal by the moment and I really didn't know quite what to do. I couldn't just leave because I had the keys and had to lock the house up, yet, on the other hand, I didn't want the embarrassment of interrupting an idyll. If Adam had come to the house, and by the moment this looked more and more likely, to find somewhere private to screw Anastasia, he wouldn't be best pleased to find me in the woodwork. As he folded her in a P.G. embrace, swiftly warming up to an X certificate embrace, I tiptoed backwards down the pantry passage, paused for a moment and then advanced noisily, whistling a jaunty air.

"Adam!" I said as I came in view. "Good Heavens! Great to see you and welcome home! We weren't expecting you till Monday."

"Jack!" he said, "Well, hi there, Jack! Well met!"

'Jack? Hi there? Well met?' What was this?

"Hurried home," he said, "to show Anastasia the house. And before we say any more, let me present Mr. Simpson, Mrs. Burbank. Annie and I got married last Sunday," and he passed an uxorious arm around the pliant Anastasia and kissed her warmly.

Did I hear a throaty, "Oh, naughty Adam!"? I believe I did.

"Ha,ha,ha!" said Adam. "You look surprised."

"I'm not surprised, I'm flabbergasted, delighted, amazed! So happy for you! Congratulations!" ("This'll shake Gary," I thought.)

We shook hands. Anastasia extended a soft and scented cheek and we set off for a tour of the house, Adam and Anastasia hand in hand, me marvelling at their side.

"Shut your eyes, Baby," Adam cooed, "and wait for the surprise!"

He threw open the door. "Our bedroom, Darling," he gargled. "And all for you!"

"Oh, Angel," said Anastasia, fluttering and dimpling, "eet ees vonderfool but - why deed you choose blue?"

Now this, if I had had eyes to see or ears to hear was a significant remark. The significance did not dawn for a day or two. After a while I excused myself (it was getting very late) and, telling Adam what to do with the key, I sped home to Lavenham and was glad to catch Byam who was just leaving.

"News!" I cried. "Big budget of news! Come down to the Pottergate and then I can tell Claire at the same time."

Their reaction did not disappoint me! I took them through the whole encounter, sentence by sentence to a chorus of, "Did she really? And what did Adam say? You don't mean it!"

And at the end I could only say, "He just rolled over on his back with his paws in the air and an expression of nauseating devotion and enslavement on his face."

I could see that Claire didn't like the idea of Anastasia very much and, indeed, she said lugubriously, "You watch that one, Jack. She sounds like trouble."

The following day there was an early morning telephone call from Adam. "Hello, Jack," he said and went on in servile, yes, servile tones, "Little change I want you to organise if you wouldn't mind. Master bedroom. Magnolia."

"Magnolia?"

"Yes, magnolia. Shade G125 on the card."

"Everywhere?" I said. "Throughout the bedroom?"

"Yes," said Adam, slightly shiftily but firmly, "everywhere."

"Okay, Adam," I said, "magnolia it is." And I proceeded to ring up Gary.

I hadn't spoken before he said, "I've heard and I've met her! She's ever so nice! Please and thank you and 'if it's not too much trouble'. Oh, no, she's all right - I can get on with her! And, I say - you know that scumble in the Big Room? You know what she said? 'I do nert like eet. Eet looks like someone 'as been seek on the vawl.'"

"Gary! For Christ's sake, you're making that up!"

"No! Straight up, Jack!" he said with I thought a good deal of satisfaction.

Short-lived satisfaction because we now moved into a curious phase. Little Anastasia, so soft, so pliable, so bosomy had a will of iron and she had Adam absolutely buttoned up. Clever colour schemes - and really Adam's colour schemes won at such a price were very clever - were dismissed by degrees and I found myself in the curious position of defending him.

"I do not like," said Anastasia one day, "the colour in the bathroom. And 'oos idea was eet to put a mirror behind the taps?"

I thought I'd give Adam a bit of a break if I could so I said, untruthfully, that it had been my idea whereas, in fact, it had been placed there deliberately so that the narcissistic

166

Adam could admire himself when he was lying in the bath. But Anastasia didn't like it and even said that it was rude.

"I'm not surprised," said Byam when I told him. "Balkan ladies are notoriously prudish."

Once or twice I remonstrated. "Adam," I said one day, "do you really want to redecorate the hall? I thought it looked damn good. Cost you a bit, you know. That silk wall lining wasn't cheap."

"I only want," came a crushed rejoinder, "little Anastasia to have it exactly as she wants."

"Adam," I said, "you're paying too high a price!"

Gary, on the other hand, was loving every minute of it and couldn't do too much to oblige Anastasia. For all the early morning and late night telephone calls, for all the changes of mind, for all the shattering public rebukes on site, he felt he was having his revenge and so did the blokes. It was suddenly Adam and me on one side, Anastasia and all the lads on the other.

"Cor," said the young ones, "nice bit of homework! These package trips to the Balkans - worth every penny, I reckon!"

"Very nice lady," said the older ones. "Polite, you know."

"Very nice and very polite to you, maybe," I said, "but she's killing him!"

And she was. Morose and apologetic, Adam Burbank watched, powerless, as his creation was inch by inch dismantled, as his Etoffes d'Antan fabrics were replaced by Poppy Saunders prints, the deep mulberry paintwork subtly picking out the backs of the shutters was covered with ICI brilliant white, the burnt sienna slate pavings were covered with Tuftigarde carpet.

"I really don't know what it's costing!" said Gary in satisfied tones.

"Well, you ought to," I said, testily. "You're the builder. If you don't know what it's costing..."

The finale came when one day - long after contract completion - I went over to inspect and found two young painters on site.

"Hello," I said accusingly, "and what are you doing here?" ('Not working under my instructions,' was my unspoken thought.)

"Redecorating bedroom 3," they said in triumphant chorus.

Bedroom 3 had been the scene of the major engagement of their war with Adam who had been seeking a colour 'somewhere on the edge between damson and dark blue'. I went to have a look. The room was now as pink as a sugar mouse. A frieze ran round below the ceiling, a frieze which displayed not a few Disneyworld characters. As I stared in disbelief, the penny dropped. Could I be the last person, I wondered, to work out the reason for Anastasia's recent embonpoint? No, even Claire hadn't worked that one out. My horrified inspection was interrupted by a throaty coo.

"Jack! Hello! What do you say now?"

I had had enough. "Anastasia, I have to tell you that I think it is quite awful! What on earth is Adam going to say?"

"'Ow can you be so stoffy? So old-fashioned! You, if you were a leetle baby, 'ow would you like to wake up in a dark purple room? Would you?"

I looked once more at the parade of imbecile, grinning faces.

"Sooner that than wake up to this lot! Think for a moment of the unborn child, Anastasia! You'll bend its infant psyche into a safety pin! You've only got to glance at Minnie Mouse to see that she's stoned out of her brains! And have you seen her shoes?"

"Aw!" she said, cuddling up to me, "you are as bad as Adam!" And, to the painters. "Isn't he?"

They agreed with her cordially. "Make a nice bright, cheerful room for the kiddy," they said.

I fled. I fell down the stairs. I banged my way into Adam's study. (The Swedish red still reigned in here.)

"Adam," I said, "I've just seen bedroom 3....!"

He looked up with lack-lustre eyes. There was a half empty bottle of Southern Comfort at his elbow.

"What are you going to do?" I squeaked.

"Have a drink," he said, tonelessly.

XVI

The Twilight Zone.

The village of Abbot's Bretton more or less writes the history of architecture for the last four hundred years. The village street is lined with substantial but unpretentious timber-framed houses. Towards the ends of the village these degenerate into early nineteenth century brick-built workmen's cottages. The rectory, a fine porticoed eighteenth century production in white Woolpit bricks remains intact as a gentrified residence though its stabling has been converted into three rather inconvenient houses with nowhere much to park.

The high ground in the village is inevitably occupied by a mediaeval church listed as being Grade A and the subject of - as the saying goes - ongoing repairs. Next door is the manor house, of all periods including an elaborate Victorian guest wing now converted to provide a wide spread of sheltered accommodation and contiguous to this is a close of executive-style residences called Periwinkle Drive. The close consists of five not quite identical 4 bed., 2 recep., 2 bthrm. (1 ensuite), dble. gge., gas c.h. dwellings with traditional detailing, the whole having a faintly Georgian flavour belied by the problems of designing sash windows of elegance against the claims of double glazing.

Something, you see, for everybody. There is even a squire, though not a resident squire. Sir George

Bedingfield, now in his eighties, lives in Antibes. Having spent his childhood in Abbot's Bretton, he returned to Suffolk after the war, didn't like what he saw, and has hardly been back since. Only a few of the remaining indigenous inhabitants have ever met him.

The village both suffers and gains from its close proximity to the county capital of which it has become an elegant dormitory. Elegant indeed! And socially stratified. At the top of the pyramid are the denizens of the timber-framed houses in the High Street with, below them, the inhabitants of the smaller nineteenth century houses and at the bottom of the pyramid, a thin layer of old inhabitants, all the tenants of Sir George, all protected and all in houses on which nothing much has been spent since nineteen thirty nine. These ungentrified houses are a considerable bone of contention. More recent incomers point the finger of eloquent and incessant disapproval at Sir George - "Those houses in Midsummer Row! A disgrace! Lets the whole village down! If Sir George isn't prepared to do anything about it, you'd think he'd sell them on to people who would be prepared to bring them up to standard."

The Parish Council occasionally write to Sir George's agent to ask what his intentions are. The reply, in various forms, is always the same - that Sir George has no intention in regard to Midsummer Row and has no intention of disturbing the present tenants. The whole situation is quite a bonding one since the socially aware parishioners can always find something to agree about amongst themselves and love to hate Sir George and his agent.

However, the vituperation to which the absent Sir George is exposed in respect of these houses is as nothing compared with that directed towards him in the matter of the village centre. As is so often the case, the village centre is, or more correctly was, occupied by a very large and now extremely dilapidated farmyard. With the advent of massive farm machinery just after the war, it was abandoned as a working farmyard. There is a fine fifteenth century barn; there is a fine sixteenth century cart lodge; cow sheds and milking parlour are well built and claim some architectural distinction, having been erected at a period of agricultural prosperity in the mid-nineteenth century. There is even a little thatched house and there are several concrete grain bins within this enclosure. Roofs sag, nettles advance, metal objects left about the place rust and there are rats. There is a pond into which incongruous things have been thrown.

You could call it a twilight zone but the children of the village much appreciate this enclosure. There are lofts, through the crumbling staircase approaches to which it would not be difficult to fall, there is a sludge pit of unknown depth in which it would be easy to drown, there is a chaff cutter on which the enterprising could cut off their fingers and there are a number of crumbling farm carts in which highly combustible straw dens can be made. The whole affair is a scandal.

Representations continued to be made to Sir George. The local authority threatened him through his agent with the law. The general thought was that the whole should be cleared away and replaced with a few more executive-style residences with their attendant patios, cupolas, boundary walling and traditional detailing, all very much in the manner of Periwinkle Drive. It was even suggested that if Sir George got on with it he could make a bomb.

But Sir George remained impervious. With childhood memories of a busy farmyard, he could not imagine the centre of the village to contain anything else. He had no personal objection to rats, he was indifferent to the suggestion that the place was dangerous. His only observation on the subject appears to have been - 'What next? Children have always played in a farmyard - did meself! Of course children are always falling off things - teaches them to be self-reliant. You might as well say all the trees in Suffolk ought to be cut down in case children were tempted to climb them! Utter nonsense!'

And so the matter rested.

However, it seemed, inevitably perhaps, that Sir George was a childhood friend of Sir Hastings. It seemed that Sir George vaguely remembered that Hastings was 'one of these architect chappies'. It occurred to him that Hastings might be able to make a few suggestions though - as was to emerge later - it never crossed his mind that Hastings might expect to be paid for this.

His letter of instruction, if it can be called that, to Sir Hastings was laconic in the extreme. After a certain amount of reminiscence and enquiry as to the whereabouts and fortunes of old friends, it ended with a single paragraph which, as far as I can remember, said this more or less:-

"I wish you'd have a look at the farmyard at Abbot's Bretton. People are always telling me I ought to do something with it. Had a letter from a chap the other day who said, 'There should be an architectural solution to the problem of this socially sensitive central village space,' whatever that may mean! See if you've got any ideas."

Sir Hastings brooded on this proposition for a while and then came and said, "Might as well look into this. What do you think? It's in a terrible mess at the moment. I understand that the parish have been pressing for ages for the total demolition of the site and its development. Not sure that that's the best idea. What we need first, of course, is a survey. Any of you chaps free?"

Of course none of us chaps was free but, as it happened, we had two schoolchildren in the office on work experience. The terrible problem with work experience people is to find them anything to do. They don't, after all, know anything about the job. They are very often not well motivated. On this occasion we had a pair whom Byam had christened Dwayne the Pain and Helpful Hannah. They seemed fairly typical but Hannah was as bright, enquiring and busy as Kirsten herself. Dwayne, on the other hand, was of the clay, earthy. Hannah had not been in the office two days before she had decided to be an architect and had begun the task of restructuring our filing system; Dwayne made no attempt to conceal that he had no ambition beyond playing football for Cambridge United.

"You'll never make a professional footballer smoking twenty a day!" said Heather acidly, bundling him out of the office to smoke in the yard for about the third time that day.

Kirsten set off with her small squad and set about the complicated survey and took an extensive set of survey photographs. After about a month in this endeavour a fine set of drawings was produced and placed on Hastings' desk where it sat, unregarded, for a week or more. I was just on the verge of urging him to do something about it when I came in one morning to find, in Hastings' spirited style, a more or less complete scheme.

Kirsten and I with Byam and Hannah settled down to view it while Dwayne nodded somnolently beside us. Attached to the drawing was a memorandum in Hastings' tiny writing.

"I understand the idea was to produce six houses with the usual trimming - four bedrooms, two bathrooms, double garage, patio garden, you name it. Don't think that's right.

"See it much more as an opportunity for social housing - affordable housing. First time homebuyers (last time homebuyers, if you like.) Chance for children born in the village to buy their own slice of it. Should be able to get twelve or even fourteen in - access is no problem as far as I can see."

This was the first time Kirsten had ever seriously seen Hastings in action. It was the first time Hannah had seen anybody in action. Both were extremely impressed. So was I. Only two of the houses had three bedrooms, the majority had two. A few had only one. No building on the site had been demolished. Even the concrete grain store had been provided with windows and a conical roof and labelled 'Gazebo'. Little flights of stairs made use of the changes in level. The barn was divided into four flats, two on the ground floor and two in the roof. External staircases led from the upper floor to gardens at a higher level. Car parking had not been forgotten - what had once been a range of pig-sties had become a range of garages. Sensibly, the little thatched house was labelled 'unallocated'. Was this caution or had Hastings' invention run out at this point perhaps?

The drawings were covered with notes saying things like -

"Another window here, do you think? There's a pretty view to the north!

"Nos. 8 and 9 just have a bed-sitting room. Call it a 'studio' on the drawings. 'Studio' indeed!

"Don't overdo the black weatherboard. Render and colour wash no. 3?" And so on.

On the back of this piece of paper he had written -

"I'm trying to create a village within a village - there must be identity. Don't want to create sanitised plots marked off in straight lines. Keep it a bit confusing - hence the little alleyway between 9 and 10 and the exit from the back of 12 to the footpath. Keep the sugar beet pad for a roller drome - better call it 'play area' I think.

"Don't let anybody persuade you not to recreate the horsepond! Call it 'Ornamental Water' on the drawing? No - call it 'Pond', that's what it is."

We set to work to produce a set of preliminary drawings assisted enthusiastically by Helpful Hannah and reluctantly or not at all by Dwayne the Pain.

Towards the end of this exercise, Hastings returned and in his cheerful way approved of all that had been done. We printed off copies and sent them to Sir George in distant Antibes. We printed off a second set and had a meeting with the planners. Disconcerted at first, they were a little bit alarmed by the density until it occurred to them that village centres do have a high density. They were, nevertheless, reasonably encouraging, attracted by the idea of what they called social housing in a village context. For the first time I began to believe there might be something in it.

Hastings dashed off an aerial perspective which we admired.

"It would have been one for Gilbert," said Hastings sadly. "I was never as good as he."

Rather annoyingly, it was more than a month before we heard from Sir George but when his letter came, it was enthusiastic. He too had hardly believed in the project until he saw the scheme and now, of course, he wanted to get on with it, asking questions that we couldn't answer about the cost, the possible returns and the marketing strategy.

The agent was dubious. "Wasn't expecting anything like this," he said. "I was thinking of something more on the lines of Periwinkle Drive. They sold very well. Think you'll be able to sell these things? This doesn't exactly maximise the potential does it? Only one bedroom? Is there a demand for that sort of thing?"

I tried to explain that I thought there were plenty of first time buyers who would be glad of a glamorous large studio and, if they'd do for first timers, they'd do for last timers. You'd get a nice mix on the site, old and young as well as families. There wouldn't be a problem getting babysitters. Young people from the village would be able to afford their own place instead of having to compete with commuters. And besides, if Sir George could sell this on with the benefit of planning consent, he'd be able to rehouse some of the tenants of Midsummer Row and spend a bit on poshing up the Row. Oh, yes, I could see it as a self-winding, self-funding, self-animating social experiment.

"Just a moment," said the agent, bemused. "Do you mind if I write that down? And, I'll tell you what - it might be tactful to send an advance copy of this to the parish council. Get 'em on your side. Have a meeting perhaps to explain what it's all about. Half of them won't be able to follow the drawings and the other half will automatically be hostile to Sir George. I'm a great believer in anticipating trouble."

So we did, indeed, send a set of drawings to the parish council and suggested they might like to meet us and talk about the scheme. I made a few enquiries as to the composition of the parish council and learned that it was, more or less, a one man band. There were half a dozen citizens on the council, it is true, but the leading hand was evidently a certain Monica Wentworth. Mrs. Wentworth, it seemed, stood in the same relationship to the parish council as Dame Shirley Porter stood to Westminster City Council. 'Whatsoever was done therein, she was the doer thereof.' She had been vociferous in her complaints about the state of the farmyard and, in our ignorant way, we had assumed that our scheme would put her instantly on our side. We were the more deceived.

Byam and I went together to address the citizenry and thought it probable that six or at most ten people would turn out to meet us. There were, in fact, thirty two so our first problem was that we'd only brought six copies of the drawings. Our second problem which was manifest from the outset was that the assembled company were irrevocably hostile. The questions came thick and fast.

"What sort of people are going to live in a place like this?" asked somebody derisively.

"Victorian rural slum!" said another.

"Well, er..." I said, in reply to the question, "first time homebuyers..."

"Single mothers," hissed somebody ominously.

"Yeah, that's right, single mothers! And we all know what that leads to - kids out of control. On skateboards. Straight down the High Street..."

"This sort of development isn't going to do much for the value of property in the village," commented a smartly dressed thirty something.

"It's going to do quite a lot to the value of property in the village," said another ominously and there was a shaking of heads.

"How much is Sir George expecting to make out of this?"

"Sir George," said Monica Wentworth, "sells off anything that will sell, neglects the remainder and then when he thinks the time is ripe sets to work to sell off the heart of the village at a fat profit for himself! Quite unsuitable! No, it seems to us that if we can't have some decent housing, housing where families could grow up, we'd do better to turn the big barn over to community use and develop the rest as a controlled open space.

"Have you or has Sir George had the CPRE advice on alternate uses for redundant agricultural buildings?" she asked with the air of one who knew them word for word. She assumed we didn't and sailed on, "Conversion to residences comes very low on the list, I can tell you! A community use - village hall or craft units is much to be preferred. A refuge for walkers or an information centre would be perfectly acceptable."

I tried to rally. "Well," I said desperately, "you've got a perfectly good village hall already and there are craft units in Bretton Magna (five still unlet) and as to refuge for walkers - well, okay, in the Yorkshire Dales perhaps but there's not much demand in muddy Suffolk and any walkers who get lost in the village tend to make straight for the Black Bull where they can get their information along with their pint of Adnams."

"Muddy Suffolk?" said someone indignantly but the landlord of the Bull sitting on the front row nodded sagely.

Somebody else chipped in, "I don't know what we want with a pond!" he said. "Won't be five minutes, if I know anything about this sort of people, before it'll be full of coke cans."

"Coke cans and condoms," said somebody in a mutter.

There was a derisive laugh.

"On the contrary," said Byam firmly, "we are proposing to have the site scheduled as an S.S.S.I."

I had no idea what he meant but I read the ominous

signs. Byam is the most peaceable citizen as a rule but he can, and he sometimes does, lose his temper and when this happens...! If he were an elephant you'd say he'd gone musth, if a large aeroplane - gone tech., if a physical body, that he'd reached critical mass or even was combusting on re-entry.

"The pond," he continued levelly, "is known to be the habitat of the Great Crested Newt."

There was a silence while this was absorbed and then someone asked, "What's an S.S.S.I. then?"

"A Site of Special Scientific Interest," said Byam. "The Great Crested Newt is a privileged citizen in rural areas. Planning Authorities go to great lengths to protect its habitat... in fact, I sometimes think that the thing to be if you live in the country is either a gypsy, a Great Crested Newt or a single mother but this scheme, as you see, caters for all three."

There was an indignant murmur which mounted to a crescendo when Byam said, "You may have noticed this little building - " He pointed to the thatched cottage, "unallocated you see at present. We thought a druggie drop-out drop-in centre might be..."

Fists were shaken. There was many a faugh of disgust. Monica Wentworth began to look triumphant. Out of the corner of my eye I noticed a citizen who was scribbling furiously.

"God!" thought I. "The press!"

I began to think our embassy had been something of a disaster.

We were eyed with baleful dislike by one and all. Opinions were divided; some had decided that we were the lackeys of Sir George - running dogs of a capitalist man-eating tiger; others thought we were whinging lefties having no regard for traditional values; some assumed that we ourselves stood to make a lot of money and others that we were hand in glove with a juggernaut developer.

At the conclusion of these stormy proceedings, Monica

Wentworth took a vote to determine what should be the parish council's reaction to our proposals.

Those in favour: 2

Those against: 28

Undecided: 2

Distributing gracious smiles around the company, Byam and I arose, collected our papers, bowed to left and right and left the room.

"You stupid wally!" I said. "You sure as hell blew that! What did you think you were doing?"

"I'm sorry," said Byam. "How can I put it? - Something snapped. I was suddenly pissed off with the lot of them. And actually, you know, I bet it won't make any difference. They couldn't see it but it's a very good scheme."

"I should think they couldn't see it! Drug drop-in centre! What next!"

"What next? I could have given them something else to think about - there's a band in the village - did you know? - called the Bretton Bombadiers. I should have said our scheme included a practice room for them..."

With many a good example still ringing in my ears I essayed a 'faugh!' of disgust.

Next day - and for weeks thereafter - the press had a ball and did not spare their comment.

"'NEWTS BEFORE PEOPLE' ARCHITECTS CLAIM." said one.

"VILLAGE CENTRE TO BECOME GYPSY CAMP," said another.

"'AIRY FAIRY ARCHITECTS ATTEMPT TO FOIST SOCIAL ENGINEERING EXPERIMENT ON HELPLESS COUNTRY VILLAGERS,' NOT IF I KNOW IT!' SAYS BATTLING CHAIRMAN, MONICA WENTWORTH.

And the leader said, "Too long has the village of Abbot's Bretton suffered under the neglect of absentee landlord Sir George Bedingfield. Sir George, unavailable for comment in his villa in Antibes, was reported at a meeting of the village council last night to be negotiating the sale (for a sum understood to be not unajacent to half a million pounds) of the ancient village centre..."

"Tell you what we've got 'ere," said Ron, "we've got a cause célèbre. Did you have a look at 'Look East' last night?"

"No I didn't," said Byam, "but I did give an interview this morning over the telephone." He looked very smug.

"Just spare me!" I said. "That's all I ask. Spare me. I do not want to hear your witty ripostes."

And so in due course we submitted a planning application and in due course a delegation of the planning committee came to inspect the site. They had received 42 letters of protest. They had received a measured letter from Sir George in which he said,

"Conservation means more than the preservation of historic fabric. It means conservation of the village way of life. This will not be achieved unless houses which old inhabitants, their sons, daughters and grandchildren can afford are made available. I am aware that the proposal now before you is not in money terms likely to be the most profitable but I do not consider this matter in money terms alone or, indeed, at all."

"Good letter," said Kirsten when she read it.

Such site visits by planning committees usually last about a quarter of an hour on site. This one lasted about an hour and a half but it served a very useful purpose, useful that is from our point of view because I could see that the planning officers and committee members were getting increasingly annoyed with the burghers of Abbot's Bretton.

"What odds are you laying, Ron?" I said, having recounted my experiences to him.

"Six to four on," said Ron, without delay. "I give evens on these occasions as a rule but I think it's better than that."

And, of course, shrewd old handicapper that he is, he was absolutely right. In a blaze of publicity, planning consent was granted. The hostility of the village rose to fever pitch. The chairman of the planning committee even received some hate mail. He was puzzled.

"Couldn't think what all the fuss was about," he said in an unbuttoned moment. "Looks like a good idea to me but what's all this stuff about a drug drop-in centre?" And, when I had explained, "Next time I'd leave your friend Alexander behind," he said indignantly. "A joke's a joke! I can enjoy a joke as well as anybody but he hasn't half given me some trouble! Still, got to raise the money, get the site sold, find a developer ready to take on this nutty scheme. Don't suppose it'll happen in my lifetime."

He was wrong. Unknown to us, Sir George had decided to involve some wealthy buddies and do the development himself.

"Good. Good," said Hastings when he heard the news. "Good chap George Bedingfield. Make a good client, I shouldn't wonder. At least he won't waste hours of our time choosing the colour of the melamine work top in the single bedroomed kitchenettes."

On account of its complexity, the drawings took a very long time. Ron was fairly free at the time and undertook many, if not to say most, of these himself and he wrote a laconic but efficient specification and in due course tenders came in and in due course the contract started on site.

The mounded rubbish of hundreds of years was extracted from the buildings. Some was sold and such is the nostalgic passion for bygones, farm implements sold very well. For the rest it seemed that for six months an enormous bonfire burned in the middle of the farmyard to the rage and fury of the immediate neighbours, notably Monica Wentworth and even at times I could find myself feeling sorry for her - she had the misfortune to live downwind of our enterprise. Her rage at the bonfire was as nothing to her rage when the crumbling and rotting remains of two ancient haystacks were ripped out. Rats emerged in very large numbers. Rats emerged and nipped across the street, taking cover as best they might in the elegant appointments of a much over-restored timber-framed house on the other side, a house on which a rough oak tablet bore the name 'Timbers', the house in which, inevitably, Monica Wentworth lived. It seemed an artistic development.

The contract moved on and time moved on too. Hannah left school and came to work for us. Kirsten suddenly seemed to be a veteran member of the firm. Transient figures passed through the office from time to time but really we had found an establishment that worked very well.

As the job drew near completion, I went over by myself one day to view the almost finished product with satisfaction. I notice several 'Sold' signs in various parts of the site; I noticed also two elderly figures in wellies and barbour jackets sitting together on a low wall and looking about them. It was a moment or two before I recognised Hastings who hailed me cheerfully, "Jack! Come and meet the boss. George, this is my partner Jack Simpson. Jack, this is Sir George Bedingfield. Turned out very well, hasn't it? Don't you think so, George?"

"Oh, yes, wouldn't mind living here meself," said George Bedingfield. "Selling well too. And so they might at the price! Shan't make a farthing out of it, of course, and I never expected to."

We set off together on a tour, George exclaiming with astonishment from time to time. "I like the way they have these little strings on the light switches - I've never seen that before. Neat sort of arrangement. What's this?"

I explained that it was a fan extractor for the kitchen.

"I say," said Sir George, "I wouldn't have thought of that. I like the way the baths have boarding round them. Much easier to keep clean. But ought they to be fitted with concrete floors? Don't like that much."

I explained that the incoming owners and tenants would have a their choice of tiles or carpeting."

"Not sure I like the idea of this bathroom. I wouldn't like

chaps coming through my bedroom to get to the bathroom."

I told him that there was a second bathroom and that this was for the exclusive use of the main bedroom.

"I say," said Sir George, much impressed, "that's a breakthrough! What are you going to call the houses?"

I said we had thought of calling them numbers 1 - 14, Bretton Yard.

"Good. Good," said Sir George, "You should see the names they've thought up for some of the houses round me in Antibes! 'Cri des mouettes', 'Le Grand Bleu', 'Prairie des fées' Huh!"

And, finally, George wandered off down the village street to call on old friends and tenants in The Row.

"Satisfied customer?" I said.

"Yes, yes," said Hastings. "Very gratifying! Well, I must be off meself. Tell you what - pop in and see me when you get back." And he too was gone.

I spent a few moments wandering round the units, a complicated bunch of keys in my hand and was just turning for Spring House myself when a car drew into the yard. From this there stepped Bill Coghill who was the selling agent. He hurried towards me.

"Oh, Jack," he said. "So glad to see you're still here. I've got a customer meeting me here to look over one of the units and somebody's got the spare set of keys. I rang your office and they said I might catch you here. May I borrow your set?"

I willingly agreed.

"Promising customer?" I asked.

"Very promising!" said Bill with satisfaction. "A member of the local parish council. Funnily enough she's had her own house on the market for years but nobody would touch it at her price while the grotty old farmyard was opposite. Now you've poshed it up it's a different ball game! Had two or three offers in fact. Funny how these things work out."

It was a while before this information sank in. A member of the parish council? Living opposite the farmyard? In a moment all was revealed. Looking grumpy, inquisitive, determined, mean and yet withall self-satisfied, who should come stepping across the road but Monica Wentworth. I wondered whether to run for cover or make myself known; whether to remind her who I was. I wondered whether she was seriously a punter. I wondered which, if any of the units she had her eye on. Curiosity got the better of me and I sidled up.

In reply to my question she said yes she was thinking of buying one of the houses. I expressed myself delighted by this turn of events, wondering if she was going to apologise for her ferocious opposition but, as I might have guessed, she had, it must be confessed, the last word.

"Yes," she said, "I'm thinking of buying number three. The view from my own house is completely ruined by all that's occurred and if I move to number three I can at least look at 'Timbers' and not have to look at all this!"

I really had to give her points.

Much gratified by these developments, I hurried back to Spring House to be greeted by Hannah. "Sir H..." (she had picked this up from Ron) "Sir H. wants to see you. They're all in there, except me." She pointed to the library.

What a surprising event! Staff meeting? We never had staff meetings. Cup of tea? Unlikely. If Hastings wanted a cup of tea he came and had one in the office. I hurried into the library.

"Well, here you are," said Hastings, beaming. "Give him a cup of tea." And to Kirsten, "Where's the whatnot, Kirstie? Ah, here we are. What do you think of this?"

He took a sheet of the familiar thick Spring House writing paper. Familiar paper but what was this? I read across the top in capitals -

MUNRO, SIMPSON & ALEXANDER, ARCHITECTS.
Jack Simpson R.I.B.A.

Byam Alexander R.I.B.A.

Kirsten Munro R.I.B.A.

Consultant: Sir Hastings Munro R.A., F.S.A, F.R.I.B.A.

Office manager: Ronald Steel L.R.I.B.A.

Practice Secretary: Heather Mills.

"There," said Hastings. "What do you think of that? Spent a long time trying to work out the batting order. 'Simpson, Alexander, Munro?' Wouldn't do - initials SAM. Don't want the firm called SAM do we? 'Alexander, Simpson, Munro - ASM? Assistant Stage Manager? Suddenly I thought of this."

I looked at Byam. He looked at me. We both looked at Kirsten.

"Did you know about this?" I said to her.

"No, I did not!" she said, pink with embarrassment. "Don't know what you think you're up to, Uncle! I can't..."

"Can't?" said Hastings cheerfully. "Course you can! Don't think these chaps could manage without you. Besides, to be quite frank with you I'm not proposing a motion, I'm issuing an instruction! Got a bit of an agreement for you chaps to sign. Better read it first. Heather could you get me the doings?"

He handed each of us a sheet of paper on which there were ten short lines. This was, in effect, a partnership deed, articles of agreement, a contract, whatever you'd care to call it. I read it cursorily. It seemed okay to me. The profit-share was generous to Byam and me and by degrees over the years Kirsten was to absorb Hastings' share. Dire words of warning so often repeated came to me, that one should never sign anything without passing it in front of a solicitor. It also occurred to me that this was for the rest of my life. I would yoke myself to Byam for the foreseeable future. Did I want this? And ambition? What had happened to ambition? I thought for a bit and decided that I had never really had any, at least no ambition that was not contained by Spring House. And Claire? What would Claire say? I hesitated no longer. I took the large and ancient fountain pen from Hastings' hand and signed an elegant black signature.

Byam followed suit. Kirsten demurred.

"I can't sign this," she said angrily. "I've hardly been here two years."

"Two years?" said Byam. "Seems longer."

He took her hand and put the pen in it. He put an arm over her shoulder. "Just sign the bloody thing!" he said.